But baby, you're worth it!

By Tamara Chavalle

NATIONAL LIBRARY OF AUSTRALIA

A catalogue record for this book is available from the National Library of Australia

Publisher:

Australian Self Publishing Group, Pty. Ltd / Inspiring Publishers
PO Box 159, Calwell, ACT 2905, Australia.
Phone: 61-(0) 2 6291-2904
http://australianselfpublishinggroup.com

National Library of Australia Prepublication Data Service

Author: Tamara Chavalle

Title: **But baby, you're worth it!**

ISBN: 978-1-923087-22-4 (print)
ISBN: 978-1-923087-21-7 (ePub2)
ISBN: 978-1-923087-20-0 (eBook)

Dedication

To mum and my beautiful babies. I can't possibly put into words how much you mean to me. I love you all. "To the whole wide world and back".

Alex Munroe, my wonderful Editor.
I can't wait to work with you again.

Table of Contents

But baby, you're worth it!

Chapter 1
Monday, 16th May, 2022

I t was the day — finally — the day I'd been waiting for, for the past 9 1/2 years. The day that I would get to meet my precious second-born, my sweet little boy. The day that my Rose would get to meet her much anticipated and longed for baby brother. The day that my mum would finally get another grandson. The day I never thought I would see. It was Monday 16th May, 2022.

I was due at the hospital at 6am. After getting everything packed months ago for a week's holiday, I had finally sat down the previous night and packed a slightly more sensible hospital bag. I'd had so much fun buying all the lovely boy's clothes and had chosen such a sweet little outfit to take my boy home in — a little grey pair of leggings and a white long-sleeve top, both from my favourite store. I had also packed his name blanket to wrap him up in. A beautiful, grey-blue blanket, my favourite colour, custom-made as a gift from two cherished friends, sisters Lindsay and Chelsea, just for my boy.

My due date was still 12 days away, but my little boy was a good size. Because of my age, I had been lucky enough to see him on ultrasounds every few weeks throughout my pregnancy. The decision to induce me at this point was one that I agreed with. They were expecting him to be at least 3.4 kilograms. I could not wait to meet my little boy.

I didn't want everyone to have to rush out of the house at 5:30 am, so I had organised for a ride-share to take me to the hospital. My mum would take Rose to school and then she'd come up to see me.

The birthing suite was in the new building, very different to the old and outdated building that I gave birth in last time, which will have been 12 years ago following month. I was met by a midwife, who took me through to my room. I got comfortable and played on my phone while I waited for the induction process to begin.

Mum arrived after school drop off, it was after 9am and the induction process had started. Nothing much was happening as the morning progressed, apart from a little pain here and there, so at lunch time, the midwife suggested I should go for a walk to see if that would help to get things started. So, Mum and I headed out to the main building of the hospital. There were several shops in the foyer, and as we wandered around, browsing in the windows it definitely felt like things were starting to happen, I was starting to get those familiar pains, it may have been nearly 12 years since I had last experienced them, but suddenly it felt like yesterday. It was a strange feeling, because although it was really starting to hurt. It excited me to think that maybe things would move quickly, I knew that this time I wouldn't have to fight for an epidural. Last time had been a pretty traumatic affair.

     But baby, you're worth it!

When giving birth to my daughter, my placenta previa hadn't moved after all. I'd started haemorrhaging, and wasn't making any progress after several hours. Through that whole ordeal I had begged for an epidural, for seven hours, but nobody had listened. By the time they finally came through, it was too late, so it didn't work. For this birth, I needed constant reassurance that things would be different, that they wouldn't make me go through hours and hours of unnecessary pain. I had tried to push for a cesarean section right from the first appointment with the doctors, because I was so terrified of a repeat of what had happened the first time, but the doctors had talked me out of it, assuring me that last time was because of the low-lying placenta. My placenta was nice and high this time and so, with the early epidural, I would have a nice, easy and pain-free labour. And so I was excited about giving birth. I was excited about the idea of being able to enjoy labour as I'd heard other women do.

We made our way back to the birth suite. I was convinced that things were starting, and I figured I should probably be in the right place for what came next. I sat down on the bed and a midwife came to examine me, but by this time, the contractions had almost stopped. I was only one centimetre dilated. I would need another round of induction gel, but it was starting to look like nothing was going to happen. Because the induction hadn't worked at that point, I was going to have to stay in for the night. I knew that there was a chance baby wouldn't arrive that day, but I had a plan.

If I didn't have him by the end of the day, I would go home and come back in the morning. Rose and I would have one of our much-loved carpet picnics for dinner, a tradition we'd started many years ago on a trip to Cairns after I had caught tonsillitis from a didgeridoo I had played in a shop, and couldn't leave the room for two days. We'd ordered room service and decided it would be fun to lay our beach towels out on the carpet and have a picnic. We turned on a movie, I couldn't tell you which one, but I'm sure Rose could. Most importantly we had such a fun evening and hence a new tradition was born, the mummy-baby carpet picnic. I was disappointed that I wouldn't get one last picnic with my girl before we became a family of three, but I knew she was in good hands with her nanna, and I reminded myself that there would be plenty more carpet picnics to be had. It just meant there would be a messy little monkey at the next one, but at least he wouldn't eat much!

By this point, Mum had headed off a while ago to pick Rose up from school. They came in for a quick visit on their way home and brought me some treats. I was impressed by the hospital food; from what I'd heard, mums-to-be and new parents get a much better deal with the food than other patients. But it was still nice to have some goodies to graze on through the night. The girls stayed for a while and it was lovely to have the company. I had brought a book to read, but I couldn't concentrate, I was far too excited. It still didn't look like baby was coming that night, so they'd have to try the drip to induce me the next morning. Apparently, that would definitely kick things off. I remember how quickly things moved once that was done last time so it looked like the little man would be coming to meet his girls the following day instead

But baby, you're worth it!

✧ ✧ ✧

But before I go any further, I feel like I should probably stop and introduce myself. My name is Tabitha Powell. I'm 47 years of age, yep, you read it right, 47. It took me a lot longer to have this little baby than it was supposed to, but I'll tell you more about that in a minute.

I live in a beautiful leafy suburb on Sydney's North Shore called Lane Cove. I've been living here since I was just nine. I may be biased, but I truly believe I live in the nicest little corner of the world. It's not just me, though. Lane Cove was voted the most livable suburb in NSW this year. You'd never know that my slice of heaven is located just a 10-minute drive from the centre of Sydney. If you're a local then you can't possibly walk around our shopping village without bumping into someone you know. Lane Cove Council incorporates 6 suburbs and all of them are within walking distance of Sydney harbour or the Lane Cove River.

I guess there are dozens of things I could tell you about my appearance. I have blue-grey eyes and long blonde hair. I'm about five foot six inches tall, and go up and down between size 10 and 12, depending on whether I'm on a health kick or a caramilk one. I was pretty once, or so I was told. Back when I used to sleep 8 hours a night and wear makeup. I guess I still scrub up okay when I make an effort, all things considered.

I love anything pink or leopard print. My taste in music is as eclectic as my sense of fashion. My favourite playlist has everything from Pink to Coffey Anderson, Kasey Chambers to

Taylor Swift and David Bowie. I'm a massive fan of tattoos and diamonds, in equal measures, I will never have enough of either. But I am even more so a fan of my small circle that is made up of my closest family and friends. I am blessed to have a truly amazing group of people who love and inspire me.

I also love clothes and accessories. I wouldn't say that I've ever been particularly fashionable, well not in a conventional way. You might call my style something along the lines of 'Inked Glam Mumma' style. One day you'll see me walking along in a nice sundress with wedges looking perfectly normal, the next day I'll be wearing a sparkly Dolly Parton T-shirt with a denim ruffled mini-skirt and rose gold cowboy boots. I've had people mock me for my strange sense of style in the past, but as I've grown older, I've come to realise that my quirky sense of style makes me happy. Being happy is one of my goals in life. That, and being able to spoil and take care of my mum and my children.

I've already got one beautiful child, as you may have already guessed, an almost 13-year-old daughter by the name of Rose. She was nearly 12 when her brother was on his way. I have loved her name since I was in high school with a girl who had the same name. Rose was pretty, sweet and popular. I also happen to love roses, they're so pretty, and nothing smells quite as sweet. I chose her name years before I even realised that I wanted to meet her. I had Rose when I was 34, realising a little later than when was ideal how desperately I wanted children.

Rose looks like my mum. They both have the same eyes as me, but they're red- heads. My skin is olive, but they both have pale

                    But baby, you're worth it!

skin. Rose is as sweet as her name suggests. My daughter is kind, generous and gentle. Animals and small children naturally gravitate towards her; she gets that from my mum as well. And she has the voice of an angel. I can hold a note or two. My car concerts are legendary. But my daughter, wow. She's been singing on stage since she was 5 and she never ceases to amaze me when I hear her voice. Rose is like a Disney princess.

I'm a single mum. Rose's father and I had a weird thing that we did on and off for about 15 years. I thought he was the love of my life. He wasn't, not by a long shot. But the little girl he gave me absolutely is. From the moment I met her I finally knew what true love was.

Rose and I live in a converted granny flat underneath my mum's house. I have lived in the same house since I was nine years old when we moved here from Kensington, over in the Eastern suburbs. Back then, it was both of my parents, myself and my two brothers. Michael is 18 months older than me and then Nick, the baby of the family, is two years younger. My mum lives in the main house with my niece, Brittany. That's a story for another time. She has been living with us since she was nine. My dad moved out when I was just 14, which was for the best. We have a happy family, if not a conventional one.

When I'm not being a mum, a daughter or a fashionista, I work in tech sales. Well, I used to, I'm taking some time off right now. I didn't grow up wanting to be in sales. I was the shy kid who hid behind my mum's dress. My shyness really held me back at school. I was so far behind by the middle of year 11 that

I dropped out, convinced that I was too stupid to catch up with my friends and other peers. My uncle Greg worked in sales and I had always idolised him. Following in Greg's footsteps seemed like the best way to make a good life for myself — so that's what I did.

Another thing I idolised about my uncle was his absolute obsession with the South Sydney Rabbitohs. It wasn't just me, though. My whole family has one green eye and one red one. My mum used to take her little brother to games when they were just kids. They'd spend the whole day at Redfern oval. I remember being no more than five or six myself and going along to Redfern with my mum, brothers, Greg and his mates. We still sit with his best mate Mark today. We'd have a wonderful time screaming at the opposition and booing at the ref. I'm pretty sure those early games are at least partly responsible for my propensity for dropping the f-word far more often than any respectable mum should. Rose has never picked up that bad habit. It's occurred to me several times throughout my pregnancy that I need to start being more careful. I doubt that I'll get two kids that don't copy what is, by far, my worst habit.

So, the last thing I want to tell you about myself, at least for now, is why I was in my mid-forties and being induced with my second baby. He wasn't one of those happy midlife accidents that you sometimes hear about, quite the opposite in fact. Rose was two by the time I felt ready to have another baby. I'd been single since I was six months pregnant with her. I wasn't interested in bringing a man into my daughter's life, or mine

But baby, you're worth it!

quite frankly and so I made the decision to go down the path of being an SMBC, or single mother by choice.

After all, I may not have initially intended to raise my daughter without a father but in the end, it had worked out beautifully. We had travelled the world and answered to no man. I didn't need to get someone else's permission the first time I took her to Disneyland, or when we spent a week in Hawaii for my 40th, just the two of us. I couldn't wait to expand my little family and continue our wonderful adventures.

It took a few months to research fertility clinics and other options. I was so grateful that I lived in a country where single women had the option of using de-identified sperm donors to help them conceive. Meaning that the men were anonymous at the time of conception but the child could, if they wished, find out who their donor was once they turned 18. There was a lot to consider when it came to searching for the right donor. You had physical features, of course, but then you had things like family medical history, intelligence and hobbies. It was more than a bit overwhelming, especially knowing the child, or indeed children, had the right to meet that donor once they were a young adult. I had to somehow choose a man who would someday do the right thing by my child, without ever having met him. I also had to really think about what traits were important to me, and which ones were nothing more than just nice to have.

I had always been a massive list maker and so before I ever saw a single donor profile I sat down and worked out what my priorities were. I eventually made the decision that the most important thing was a healthy baby. I knew that I wanted the child to look like my daughter and so I decided that I would choose physical characteristics that were similar to those of the man who had helped me to create her. Of course, I had often joked that he had ended up being nothing more than a sperm donor, but I realised, while going through the process of choosing those traits that were most important to me, that the men who donated their genetic material to help a total stranger create a human, knowing that they would have no say in the way the child was raised or indeed any kind of relationship with them, were completely different and far more kind and honorable men than the one I had made my beautiful daughter with.

At first, I actually considered adopting. I thought that bringing a child into our family who was already on this earth and in need of a loving family was a wonderful idea. Then I started researching the process. The more information I found, the more disheartened I became. Not only was there a massive amount of money required upfront just to put your application in, there was no guarantee that you would be matched with a child to adopt. The average wait time was seven years, and most countries that allowed Australians to adopt children did not allow single parents. They would rather leave little children in orphanages than let loving single parents raise them. I will never understand how that makes any sense. It still makes me angry all these years later.

But baby, you're worth it!

I wasn't sure how the cost of almost $10k, Aussie that is, just to apply to adopt was at all fair or justifiable. I was lucky that financially I was in a good position. I was making good money in my sales career and my mum and I had purchased a tiny beach side property a couple of hours north of Sydney some 20 years earlier.

The beach cottage had finally been paid off a few months before I started researching my options. My share of the small income from that cottage was the reason I was able to even entertain going down the path of having more children. I had talked to so many women on different forums that had needed to use their superannuation or who had taken out loans to realise their dream of having children. It was horrible and so very unfair.

Adoption within Australia is extremely rare, with only around 200 children adopted in any one year, and most of those were to people who'd had to foster and say goodbye to several children before actually being able to adopt. I wasn't willing to let my little girl bond with another child as a sibling, only to have them taken away. And so finally, when my baby was almost three, I marched myself off to the fertility clinic. I was ready to get knocked up. I had managed to get pregnant with Rose on the very first try and so I fully expected the same thing to happen for my second baby.

I wasn't particularly worried when the AMH test, which measures a woman's remaining egg reserves, came back to say I had less eggs than was normal for my age. I was confident that I was going to get pregnant quickly despite those pesky test results.

I had never intended to do IVF, that was for infertile people. All I needed to do was a round of intra-uterine insemination, IUI or "the turkey baster", as I'd often heard it referred to in movies. I had wanted to do a natural cycle, without fertility drugs, but in the end, I agreed to the hormone injections because of the low egg count. I had it in my mind that I was going to hop along and get myself pregnant with twins and knew that I had a better chance of that happening with the hormones which would cause multiple eggs to be released when I ovulated.

I was planning to have two more babies, after all, so I figured I might as well have those babies in one go. I was shocked, but not at all discouraged, when the first cycle didn't work. By the third failed cycle, I was angry. The specialist I had chosen was careless, treating me like a number rather than a human being. I knew that she wasn't timing my inseminations properly and so I moved to a new clinic that was closer to home.

Those three cycles of IUI marked the beginning of a nine-year journey to try to have another baby. I was 37 when I started, a perfectly acceptable age to have a baby. I was going to stop at 40, but that milestone came and went far too quickly. With every year that passed, my desire to have another sweet little baby and to give my Rose a sibling continued to burn like a fire in my empty belly. Using both local and US recruited deidentified sperm donors, I managed to get pregnant four times before this baby, but they never lasted long. My doctors —and there were many over those nine long years — would tell me that it was my eggs, that quality was the issue. I knew better though, and so after that fourth miscarriage I pushed for answers.

     But baby, you're worth it!

A friend of mine had told me to get tested for something called natural killer, or NK cells. If the levels of those cells were too high your immune response would kick in and your body would basically attack an embryo, seeing it as a threat to the body. I was not at all surprised when my levels came back far higher than they should have been. I have all kinds of autoimmune issues. I have psoriasis and severe food intolerances, among other things. Knowing about my autoimmune issues should have prompted the doctors to test me years ago. Maybe I could have finished my family earlier, maybe not. All I know is that when the discovery of those NK cells was made, I had 2 perfect 5AA embryos frozen in storage.

There still wasn't a lot known about the effectiveness of using drugs to shut down the immune system, to combat Natural Killer cells, but as soon as I was given the diagnosis, I was determined to try it. I had always believed that knowledge was power and so I researched my heart out. I decided that if my newest fertility specialist, at the same clinic where my little embryos were frozen in the lab, was not willing to put me on an immune protocol then I would find another doctor who was. Thankfully, she was willing to give it a go, although with a much gentler protocol than the one I had researched and asked her about.

The immune protocol involved two different courses of antibiotics, which would be started two weeks before the embryo was due to be transferred. I was to start prednisone, an oral steroid, at the same time. The purpose of the medications was to shut down my immune system so that it wouldn't attack the embryo. I would also need to do all of the normal hormone medications for a frozen embryo transfer, and then I would start blood thinning injections the evening of my transfer. It was overwhelming — but I was willing to do whatever I could to finally have my second child, or to at least know that I had tried absolutely everything.

Of course, Covid messed things up and added a fair chunk of time to my journey. Our lives were all being put on hold in so many ways, but not being allowed to go ahead with IVF for all those months was so very frustrating. I finally had a real chance of bringing home another baby so each month that my period came and went during the lockdowns was brutal. I was one of so many women and parents-to-be that were waiting in limbo because IVF was considered as some kind of luxury instead of the urgent medical treatment that it was.

There were thousands of us who were forced to wait because our treatments were classed as elective surgery. IVF is not a luxury, though. No one chooses to go down the assisted conception route to have their children. It was horrible, invasive and often impersonal, it was nothing like the luxury of getting pregnant naturally, at least not in my experience. Finally, several months after the pandemic started the rules changed and IVF was finally allowed to go ahead again.

But by then my body had decided it was ready to start perimenopause. My periods stopped in April 2021. By July, my Fertility Specialist decided that we would have to start hormone replacement therapy to bring on my period so that I could start my cycle. Thankfully, the HRT worked and in August 2021, I was

But baby, you're worth it!

allowed to start my cycle. After two weeks of taking the cocktail of medications, I was finally knocked up.

I went through hell and back to have my baby boy. I had endured all those years of fertility treatments, painful procedures to remove endometriosis and flush my tubes. I had gone through the heartbreaking miscarriages — and then there were the medical bills that totalled almost $100k. All of it was part of the adventure that led me to that moment, the moment that I was finally about to meet my baby boy.

Chapter 2
Tuesday, 17th May, 2022

That night, I slept soundly. I was exhausted from the anticipation of the day before. Now it really was the day. Monday had turned out to be the practice run, but that day, Tuesday 17th May, it was happening for real. I would get to meet the beautiful little man who'd been kicking up a fuss for the past few months.

I recalled the first time he really made himself known was at Rose's end-of-year concert at the opera house the previous year. Apparently, he loved good music, because at only around 17 weeks, I felt my little fellow dancing around. I don't remember what piece of fruit he resembled at that point, but I know that it was much earlier than I'd felt Rose. I remember sitting in that pink theatre at the Sydney Opera house, in my blue wraparound dress, so excited that the tiniest little bump was starting to appear, wondering if I was imagining it, but knowing that it was real, that my little fellow was already making it known that he liked that girl he was soon to meet. His girl, who I was sure was about to become his best friend.

I jumped out of bed at around 5:30am, I was used to waking up at that time to get everybody ready for school and work so

I rarely needed an alarm. Everything was so rushed and chaotic when I went into labour with Rose because of the hemorrhaging. I had been lying on the lounge happily watching *Sex in the City* when suddenly I had felt a pop. The pop had been followed immediately by a huge gush of blood. My mum had rushed me to the hospital, and I had needed to be induced as a matter of urgency. I had looked as awful as I felt that day.

This time around things were going to be different, I was going to be like those women on TV and social media who look positively picture-perfect and glowing for that first picture with baby. I grabbed my make up bag, popped in and had a quick shower and spent lots of time applying my face. Just as I was happy with my perfectly lovely appearance in the mirror, a nurse walked in. She kindly stopped herself from laughing... I'm sure that walking in and seeing a big, round, heavily pregnant woman all made up and looking like she was ready for a first date must've been quite a sight at 6am. I'm glad I gave her a giggle. Once I was back in bed, I was checked over and told that the nurses would be in by around 7am to get me into my birthing room to get things started.

Back at home, the morning was shaping up to be like any other. Rose had been so excited about going to the Morgan's place for the day. The Morgans are the parents of one of my best friends, Tina, my longest time friend. In fact, we've known each other since we were just 10 years old, more than 35 years. We met in primary school and our families are more like family to each other. We always spent special birthdays together, we celebrated holidays and lots of other occasions whenever possible. Rose was planning to cook, bake and discuss all sorts of topics with Cathy and Brian, she's wise beyond her years, that smart girl of mine, she will go far in life.

The Morgans had finally become grandparents for the first time just 10 days earlier. They'd always loved spending time with my girl, and she had been their surrogate grandchild. It was such a relief, knowing that Rose had something wonderful to look forward to while she waited to meet our little boy.

By 9am my girl had been left in the caring and capable hands of the Morgans. A quick cup of tea and chat about all the wonderful grandbabies and mum was back at the hospital with me. The midwives were lovely, they'd been so kind and understanding about my fears about the pain. I had wanted the cesarean at first but the doctors had talked me out of it and so we had agreed that I'd be given an epidural as soon as they started the drip to get my contractions happening. I was so thankful that Rose wasn't at the hospital. I was not expecting any issues but I didn't want her to be traumatised, I didn't want her to feel scared or helpless if anything went wrong, like it had with her birth.

By the time the contractions started to become regular, the epidural had well and truly kicked in. I was thoroughly enjoying the experience, suddenly labour was a piece of cake. It was fun, talking and joking with my mum and the midwives that came in. I couldn't tell you any of their names, but they were all lovely, and so encouraging. I had expected a lot of negativity around my age. There was no such negativity, though. Everyone I'd

But baby, you're worth it!

encountered over the last eight-and-a-half months — whether it was doctors, midwives, my wonderful and supportive friends and family, even total strangers — were all absolutely lovely and so supportive. Maybe there was some judgement happening behind my back, but honestly, I had been waiting such a long time for this opportunity. I really couldn't have cared if that had happened.

After maybe a couple of hours, one of the midwives checked and asked me if I could guess how many centimetres dilated I was at that point. Trying to be conservative I think I said five or six, but she was quite excited to inform me that I was fully dilated, and it was time to start pushing. We started things off in the usual manner and things were going well. The epidural meant that the experience, although uncomfortable, was certainly not painful. Until about half an hour after I started pushing. The epidural had worn off, and suddenly I could feel everything.

During my pregnancy, every time I'd had a scan, my little guy was always waving his tiny hand, just like Rose had done. He liked to hide his face and try to keep some mystery in the relationship. As it turned out, he had decided he was going to be born with his hand on his face, meaning his elbow was sticking out, making it difficult for him to progress through the birth canal. As I was waiting for the anesthetist to come in and sort out the epidural situation, suddenly there seemed to be some fussing going on with the midwives.

I had been pushing for an hour at this point, baby was stuck, and as it turned out, he had now pooed in his waters. The midwives kept talking about how they needed to do anything they could to avoid a caesarean. They talked about using forceps instead. I'd needed vacuum assistance when giving birth to Rose, so I didn't hesitate when they shoved a form in front of me to sign, saying that forceps were a safe way to deliver the baby, safer than a caesarean. All of this was happening while I was in an immense amount of pain. I kept thinking that surely, they should just do a c-section after all, but then I figured I should just trust them to do what was best. They were the ones who knew what to do. They'd get my baby out safely.

But baby, you're worth it!

Chapter 3

Tuesday, 17th May, 2022 - Continued

The decision was made to deliver my baby with forceps. Within minutes of signing whatever that form was, I was rushed off to theatre. By that point the epidural was working again but I had watched enough medical shows to know that meconium, i.e. where the baby had done a poo in his waters, was not safe for the baby if it was swallowed or inhaled, and so I was eager for them to get him out as soon as possible. With some help from the midwives, I was moved onto an operating table, and I remember the anesthetist talking about a stronger anesthetic to make sure I couldn't feel anything.

I was feeling quite anxious by that point, but Mum had been given scrubs and was sitting next to me holding my hand. I was numb from the waist down, so when the obstetrician quite angrily demanded that I needed to push harder, I had no idea whether I was able to do that, but I tried with all my might.

After what seemed like a lifetime, but was probably only a couple of minutes, I heard the beautiful sound of my little baby screaming his lungs out. He was placed on my chest, and I cried, tears of joy, laughing and crying as this new baby boy tested his lungs for the first time. He screamed about the injustice of being pulled from his nice, warm, happy place. He was here, my little Max.

The tiny, wriggly, pink boy, with his mum's lungs, was here at last. I was relieved that the stronger anaesthetic had worked, I hadn't felt the forceps or any more of the contractions. I'd had a lovely pain-free labour and for that I was so very thankful.

One of the midwives came over and took Max. Thankfully, Mum walked off with them, so she was able to take pictures of him being weighed and measured. He was not happy about the cold new place that he'd been thrust into. There was nothing like making a new human to keep you warm, so I hadn't noticed that it was actually quite chilly in the operating theatre. It had been chilly for weeks, winter had come early and so, lying there in his birthday suit on the cold scales did not go down well.

Max screamed and screamed, but finally, he was cleaned up, with a nappy on and a blanket snuggly wrapped around him, and he was handed to his Nanna. She had been the first one to cuddle Rose and, once again, she was instantly in love with her new grandbaby.

By then I had completely forgotten about my perfect makeup, applied some eight hours earlier. I did have to giggle later, when I realised that my makeup had completely worn off. I had noted to myself for next time that I would probably be better off waiting until after baby was out to do my face. Although the

But baby, you're worth it!

thought of doing anything of the sort at that moment seemed absolutely ridiculous.

I had to have a fairly substantial episiotomy, and I'd also torn so the doctors were working frantically to try and get me all stitched back up. Something was mentioned about significant blood loss, but it didn't really hit home until I was finally being wheeled out of the room. I looked over to the table where I had delivered my little Max, and it looked like a crime scene. I was horrified.

I knew that I had lost almost a litre of blood when I gave birth to Rose and apparently the same thing had happened this time. The difference was that last time I had not actually seen the blood all over the floor. At that point though, the epidural, or spinal block as I was later told, was still well and truly working so nothing about that blood really concerned me. I figured it must be normal.

Mum had to race off once I was all stitched up to go and pick up Rose from the Morgans. I figured she would go home and feed the animals as well as it was getting late, but she raced Rose straight back to meet her new baby brother.

It was less than an hour after Max had arrived that I was lying in recovery. Max was in the plastic bassinet next to my hospital bed, fast asleep, absolutely exhausted from the ordeal of being born. Mum and Rose arrived at the hospital. Only one person was allowed into the recovery area to visit at a time so Mum sent Rose in: it was her turn to meet her new little brother.

Rose tentatively walked in, between the curtains that gave me some privacy from the rest of the patients in recovery, not wanting to disturb me should I be sleeping. But I was wide awake, just staring at my tiny boy in awe and waiting for his big sister to arrive. I couldn't wait for her to meet him. As she made her way over to the bed, a little unsure about it all, she gave me a big hug and kiss. It felt like a lifetime since I'd seen her, in reality it had been less than 24 hours. So much had happened since we were last together though, now it was time for my sweet girl to meet this new baby. Our baby. Max.

My first-born made her way over to the bassinet to the left of me. Little Max was still sleeping peacefully. He looked like a tiny porcelain doll. As soon as his girl laid eyes on him, she was overcome with emotions. She burst into tears, they were happy tears. It was absolute love at first sight. I knew the feeling well. I'd felt the same way when she was born. That huge rush of love that overtakes you.

I'd been in love before and it was lovely, but it also filled you with uncertainty, it made you crazy, sometimes in a good way but often not. But this was different, it was absolutely the purest and deepest love I'd ever known. I was in awe of that new little person. I knew from the first moment I held her that I would do anything to keep her safe. I would lay down my life for her, without a second thought.

I had often wondered whether it was possible to love another child the way I loved my sweet Rose. But the moment my little boy was placed on my chest I learned that it was absolutely

But baby, you're worth it!

possible. I felt the same way I had on that day, nearly 12 years earlier. And so, watching my baby girl, crying those tears of joy as she ever so gently touched the cheek of our sweet little boy, I knew that she had just fallen in love for the first time. My heart swelled with pride.

As Rose continued to marvel over her boy, a couple of the midwives who'd been in the room for the first part of my labour, before I was rushed to theatre, came to check in and see how I was feeling. They'd been the ones who had realised I wasn't going to get Max out without help. They'd heard about the blood loss and the massive tearing and cutting that had been done and were worried about me. They were also relieved that Max had been delivered safely. There had apparently been a lot of meconium leaking and they had been really worried that it could have been harmful or even fatal for my baby.

I had really enjoyed chatting with them during the early stage of my labour and I felt honoured that they would want to come to check on me. I didn't truly understand all the fuss about Max until that moment, but I still didn't understand why they were concerned about me. I was tired, sure, but I wasn't in any pain. I knew that there would be a bit of discomfort for a couple of weeks while the stitches healed, I remembered that all too well from last time, but at that moment I was just happily numb. I'd worry about the discomfort when it started. I was far too busy being in love with my new baby to care about anything else.

As the midwives turned to take their leave another couple of people came into my curtained-off area of the recovery room, one of whom was the doctor who'd delivered Max. He was there to talk me through what had transpired during the delivery. He'd had to do an episiotomy in order to use the forceps but I'd ended up tearing quite significantly, something about a 4th degree cut, or was it the tear? I wasn't sure, he was talking so quickly and I was tired so it was hard to keep up.

My placenta had broken away so they'd had to manually remove some of it. The same thing had happened with Rose but he didn't seem to know that when I mentioned it. It was common knowledge, at least from what I'd read, that once you'd had that issue with the placenta breaking away, it was very common to have it happen with future births. It was all over my medical records, I'd discussed it extensively with the doctors who'd seen me throughout my pregnancy and it was a part of the reason I'd needed to see the obstetrician rather than a midwife. I had been classed as high risk, in fact.

But it was okay, they'd sorted it out, just like last time. There had been a substantial amount of blood loss. That part I already knew. I'd heard them talking about it when they were stitching me up but I'd also seen the blood all over the floor. I'm not sure how they measure blood loss when it's all over the floor, but somehow, they do, and he said that I had lost 900ml. I'd had a postpartum hemorrhage, and he said that they would need to keep an eye on the bleeding to make sure it eased off. Once again, it was the same as last time. I'd lost exactly the same volume of blood with Rose.

          But baby, you're worth it!

None of the news worried me, it really was very similar to last time and at least I hadn't felt everything as it was happening, unlike last time. Rose's birth had left me with PTSD. It had been a horrific experience. It had been 12 hours of absolutely agonizing hell and then to top it all off she hadn't made a single noise. From the moment she was born, I didn't hear a single scream or even a whimper. I still remember the absolute terror I felt, wondering what was wrong with her. I remember asking if she was okay. As it turned out, she just wasn't a screamer. She was just lying there taking it all in, she's still like that today, cool as a cucumber.

I healed quickly last time, although emotionally it was a longer journey because it had been such a long and painful experience. That's why I was so desperate to get the epidural early for my second labour. It meant that the mental scars could be avoided, and I was so very thankful that they had. Apart from that half an hour when I was first pushing, I had felt no pain at all. We'd had a scare when Max pooed in his waters but he had arrived, safe and sound. Still sleeping beautifully beside me, my sweet little dolly.

Once the doctor had finished explaining all of the complications that had come up and been dealt with, he left the room. I never saw him again. It was only in hindsight, sometime weeks later, that I came to understand that doctor's concern, and the stern conversation we were having.

Chapter 4
Tuesday, 24th May, 2022

Those first couple of days after Max was born were a bit of a blur. I was relieved to find that everything came back to me just as I had assumed it would. Someone I'd spoken with in a social media forum had tried to warn me that I would surely have forgotten everything about having a newborn after so many years.

I'd then been given the same warning from a young male doctor I had spoken to during a routine iron infusion that I'd needed about 30 weeks into my pregnancy.

I brushed their comments off, though. When I'd given birth to Rose, I was about as clueless as they came. I mean, not three men and a baby clueless, but I was no Mary Poppins either. I figured it all out though. I was a pro at changing nappies in no time. The first few baths had been more than a bit terrifying but I'd got the hang of it before too long.

Rose had an incredible amount of strength in her neck and so that part wasn't as scary as it could have been. I had every bit of confidence that I would remember everything and I assumed that anything I had forgotten would surely come back to me.

  But baby, you're worth it!

When my baby boy needed his first nappy change, I had a moment, I won't lie, where I panicked briefly about whether I was doing it properly. But just like I had done almost 12 years earlier, I figured it out.

I was immediately capable of holding, changing, bathing and just so completely loving my sweet, handsome, little boy. I was surprised by how much my stitches hurt, but I knew that I had only just given birth. I knew from the first time that I was looking at a week or two of discomfort. I couldn't remember the same level of pain the first time, not once the actual labour was over, but I pushed it aside.

The one thing that didn't come easily though was attempting to breastfeed.

The experience of trying to breastfeed Rose whilst dealing with the extensive amount of cutting and tearing that I'd endured, as well as the complete lack of sleep had contributed to the PTSD that I had ended up battling for more than a year after her birth and I vowed that I was never going to try doing that again.

Of course, that all changed when I gave birth to my tiny Max. When he was placed in my arms for his first feed I didn't hesitate to try and feed him. I'd completely forgotten about the tin of formula and bottles that were packed in my hospital bag. In an instant, I had forgotten all about that first disastrous attempt to feed my daughter. Most of the midwives were lovely and gentle and most were patient. Feeding your babies was something that should come naturally to a woman, but that had not been my experience and so they were so very reassuring.

By day two it became clear that I was once again going to fail at feeding my baby. I was disappointed, but I was also proud that I'd at least had the courage to try. I was due back at work less than three weeks later anyway, and so I realised that it was probably for the best. A couple of days after bringing Max home from the hospital I realised that my milk was coming in but by then I had established a good routine with bottle feeding and so I decided to let it dry up. Within a couple of days, the milk was all but gone and so it was pretty clear that I had made the right decision.

A day or two later, I noticed that my baby boy's eye was looking a bit weepy. I knew straight away that my little Max had a blocked tear duct. Rose had the same problem as a baby, in the same eye. I knew that his eye needed to be flushed and so I immediately jumped into action. I grabbed some sterile water and cotton wool and gently wiped under the eye, towards his tiny nose.

When Rose had the blocked tear duct as a baby I had panicked and raced her straight to the doctor. My GP had shown me how to gently bathe the eye, and within a few days the blockage had cleared. I wasn't at all worried about Max developing the same issue in those early days, not at first at first anyway. After a couple of days, I noticed that his eye was not getting better. It had also started to look quite red.

                    But baby, you're worth it!

By the third day, I was really starting to worry. I knew that the blockage was getting worse and we needed to get some ointment to sort it out. I was still not feeling anywhere near ready to drive, so Mum drove us up to the chemist after we had dropped Rose at school. I had used the ointment for Rose a few times over the years and so I was confident that everything would be fine within a couple of days. I knew the pharmacist, Melinda, well, and she was aware of my long journey to have my little boy. I'd been buying all of my fertility drugs from her for several years.

After exchanging pleasantries, I explained to Melinda what was happening but she informed me that she would need a letter from the GP or midwife giving her authority to dispense the ointment for such a tiny baby. As it turned out, babies under two years of age needed a medical practitioner to approve the medication or the chemist could not sell it to me. I was a little flustered, worried about my baby's eye. The small amount of harmless-looking discharge had started to look pussy. It was a Tuesday and so our GP was closed. I realised I would have to go home and get the phone number I'd been given in case I had any questions I needed to ask the midwives where I'd given birth.

I thanked Melinda and grabbed a bag of those delicious chemist jelly beans before heading back over to the car, picking out and eating my favourite blue beans as Mum drove us home. We arrived home a few minutes later with a hungry and smelly baby. I carefully unclipped my tiny boy from his capsule and carried him inside. Half an hour later, I handed my clean and happily full boy to my mum so that I could call the midwives. I dialled the number in my blue baby record book and was connected with a young woman. I explained what had been happening and what the pharmacist had said, that I needed her approval to buy the ointment for Max.

The midwife explained that she would need to speak with an obstetrician before giving me the thumbs up to use the ointment on Max's eye. In the meantime, she suggested that I should bathe his eye with breast milk. I could hear that the midwife was very young and so I appreciated her due diligence. She explained that she would need to check in with the doctor and then call me back shortly. I ended the call and walked into my bedroom to retrieve the syringes that a midwife had given me weeks earlier, in case I decided to try and collect colostrum for the early days of my baby's life. I had insisted then that I had no intention of breast feeding but she had given me a knowing look and suggested I take them just in case.

I hurried to the bathroom desperately hoping that there was some milk that hadn't yet dried up but to my distress there was nothing more than a drop.

I swallowed my disappointment and headed back out to the kitchen to get a start on the housework, which had piled up since I had given birth. I decided to start with washing the dishes. Max had fallen asleep and so I knew that I had probably half an hour to get a few things done.

I should have been resting, I was not feeling good at all. I was starting to wonder if something out of the ordinary had

But baby, you're worth it!

happened when I gave birth. I was in so much pain, far more than I had been at that point with Rose. But my house wasn't going to clean itself and so, as I had been doing for the past few days, I pushed the pain aside and focused on the messy kitchen instead.

I had been cleaning for maybe 20 minutes when my phone buzzed. Not wanting to wake the baby I grabbed the phone and headed out to the back patio to take the call. I answered cheerfully, expecting to be given the go-ahead to purchase the ointment. The voice on the other end of the phone was much more serious than when I'd spoken with her just minutes before. I listened with growing confusion as she explained that I needed to bring my baby to the hospital. The doctor had been concerned about Max's eye and wanted to have a quick look before they gave him anything for it. The midwife explained that we may be at the hospital for a couple of hours and so I should bring a bottle and a few nappies, just in case.

By the time I ended the call I was in a panic. Max had just woken from his cat nap and so after explaining the situation to Mum I raced to get formula, bottles, clothes and blankets. It was absolutely freezing and so I grabbed a thick jumper for myself as well, an oversized dusty pink jumper I'd been wearing almost around the clock, only taking it off to wash it, since it was the only jumper that actually fit me, with my big belly that was only slightly smaller than it had been before Max was born.

By 11am the three of us were piled into the car, ready to get little Max sorted out before Rose finished school a few hours later.

I had been instructed to head straight up to the maternity ward, the same part of the hospital that we had been discharged from just days earlier. I wheeled Max into the hospital in his pram. I was in so much pain that I was worried about carrying him all the way from the car, but he hated it and he screamed all the way through the car park, in the lift and into the ward.

By the time we reached the receptionist that I had been told to report to, the poor little fellow was in a right state. Once I had reported to the midwives at the desk I carefully sat down in a nice, soft chair nearby and took my little Max out of his pram. As soon as he was in my arms, he cooed happily.

Within a matter of minutes, Mum, Max and I were being led along a corridor and into a treatment room. I started to become quite stressed about being in the hospital. Like most people, I hate hospitals. But thankfully, the midwives were lovely, one in particular. I wouldn't remember her name if you paid me, but she had an Irish accent and she was so sweet and reassuring. There was nothing to worry about she told me, the doctors had just wanted to make sure that Max's eye was not infected. I didn't want to be there but I didn't want to risk my baby losing his eyesight or something equally terrible.

A couple of doctors came into the room. The more senior doctor was a man who looked to be about 35. It struck me how extremely good looking he was, at first, I was amused by the fact that Max had done a wee all over me just before the doctors walked in. There I was in my huge maternity track pants, pink jumper with the big wet patch on the front of it and a messy

But baby, you're worth it!

bun in my hair with not a scrap of makeup on. I don't think I had ever looked so atrocious in public in my entire life and there I was in front of Dr Hottie.

My amusement was fleeting though. Within moments of those two doctors walking into the room, the lovely woman and her attractive colleague, I was given some shocking news. They suspected that Max had picked up an infection in his eye. Such an infection in an older child or adult was not overly dangerous but a newborn baby didn't have some membrane that protected their brain. A simple infection in the eye could easily travel to my baby's brain and cause a catastrophic situation. I started to panic then. I had no idea that something so terrible could happen. I thought my baby simply had a blocked tear duct.

Vernix is the waxy substance that protects the baby's skin for all those months they spend floating in their amniotic fluid. When Max was born the vernix wasn't completely wiped out of his right eye. Mum had mentioned it to the midwife but she had brushed it off and continued what she was doing, saying something about it being normal and fine. When I first noticed the weeping in his eye, I had put it down to the fact that his eye hadn't been wiped properly. But being told that my baby may have a nasty infection in that eye made me feel like a terrible parent. I had been so blasé about it, thinking it was nothing to worry about. Suddenly, I was being told that my baby was in danger. My tiny boy needed to be put on IV antibiotics immediately to make sure that the suspected infection did not travel to his brain.

The mere thought of my tiny baby having one of those nasty needles put in his hand was the end of me. I cuddled my little boy like my life depended on it until Dr Hottie returned with 3 nurses to insert the cannula. I was beside myself by that point. As the doctor got everything ready, I began to cry. It started as a sniffle and a silent tear but within moments I was bawling my eyes out.

One of the nurses asked me if I wanted to wait outside whilst they inserted the needle. I didn't mean to, but I snapped then, I was outraged at the suggestion. My little boy needed his mummy there. He needed to know that I wouldn't leave him. I couldn't look at the needle but the doctor had reassured me that it was tiny, nothing like those horrible things that were used for adults.

Once everything was ready to go, Max was given oral sucrose. I was told that it was an effective way to stop babies from feeling pain. As the nurse administered the sucrose, and the doctor inserted the cannula in my son's tiny hand, I bawled again. I felt like the biggest failure. I was glad that Mum wasn't there in that moment. She had gone to pick Rose up from school. I didn't want her to see me in that state, it would have worried her too much. But through all of it my tiny little warrior boy didn't even flinch. I was so grateful for that. He was so much braver than me.

By the time Mum and Rose got to the hospital we had been moved to a room in the children's ward. My tiny boy was connected to all sorts of drips and monitors and I had been given the devastating news that he would need to stay the

But baby, you're worth it!

night. I was thankful that I would at least be able to stay with him. Poor Rose was so scared when she walked into the room and saw her sweet baby brother in the hospital crib. He was so tiny that he had been placed sideways in there. He looked so fragile in that crib, but eventually she walked over and stroked his little face, ever so gently. She was conscious of his sweet little eye, careful not to touch it.

Mum had brought a tin of formula, a change of clothes for me and a few other things for Max. The nurses had given me a heap of bottles, sterile water and nappies, they had observed how distressed I was and had jumped in to try and make things a bit easier. I hadn't wanted to stay in the hospital, but I was terrified of what would happen if I tried to take Max home. The doctors had insisted that they needed to run dozens of tests to figure out what kind of infection my baby boy had in his eye. I was still convinced that he just had the blocked tear duct that I had originally suspected. I ignored my instincts and allowed them to continue running tests, whilst pumping my little baby full of antibiotics and God knows what else.

Max had been an amazing sleeper up until that point. Rose had been a stage 1 clinger as a newborn. Whenever she was put down, she would cry. She would only sleep in my arms in those first few weeks but Max would happily sleep five hours at a time in his bassinet. While we were in the hospital, he was woken up on average every two hours, sometimes more often. None of the tests run that first day had come back positive for infection but the hospital staff were convinced that something sinister was going on.

Early on the second morning, I noticed the sound of the child in the room next door. I had never heard such a horrible sound in my life. In my sleep deprived stage, it didn't occur to me to ask the nursing staff what the horrific noise was. For hours that poor little soul cried and coughed. It was heartbreaking, but it was also terrifying. I had brought my tiny boy into hospital because of his sore eye and suddenly he was being exposed to all sorts of nasty things. I didn't want to be rude, but I made sure our door was shut, nice and tight. I cringed every time I heard the poor little thing coughing or crying out. But I kept my mouth shut.

I was starting to worry about the amount of pain I was in by that point as well. The doctors had realised pretty quickly upon Max's admission that I was not doing as well as you would expect by nine days post-partum. On that second day, one of the obstetricians came in to tell me that the midwives were keen for me to go and see them to get checked out. Mum was in the room, having come back to the hospital as soon as she had dropped Rose at school that morning, but I didn't want to leave my little baby.

As the hours passed, I was becoming more and more paranoid about being kept in the hospital. Whenever I had to fetch hot water to warm up a bottle for Max when Mum wasn't in the room, I would run to the parents' room and back. I was convinced that someone was going to walk into our room and steal my baby if I wasn't there to protect him. I had fought so hard to have my sweet baby and I wasn't going to just let someone take him.

 But baby, you're worth it!

Eventually, though, I gave in. I knew the amount of pain I was feeling wasn't normal. And so, with the promise from Mum that she wouldn't leave his bedside, I headed down to the maternity ward, two floors below. Within minutes I was taken in to see one of the senior home visit midwives. The midwife seemed pleasant enough at first. She was a thickset woman in her early 50's. I was ushered over to a bed but told to sit. The bed was quite low so my feet touched the ground with no trouble. I was wearing a pair of rose gold ankle boots which I went to unzip but the midwife told me to keep them on, at least for the time being.

I was asked a number of questions about how I was coping with my baby. I explained that he was beautiful and so very loved, I talked about his nanna, his adoring sister, cousins, uncles and aunty. About how he had taken me so many years to bring into the world. But something told me that the stranger in front of me didn't believe me. I had burst into tears you see, before I'd even spoken a word. I was scared, my baby was in hospital, I was being told that he had some kind of infection that could kill him if it travelled to his brain.

I wasn't just scared. I was bloody terrified. I was convinced that something was going to happen to my tiny son and I blamed myself for not bringing him to the hospital sooner. But somehow, that woman had decided, after talking to me for 5 minutes, that I was depressed. She even tried to tell me that I had postnatal depression. And she told me that I was being ridiculous, of course I was in pain, I had only given birth 10 days earlier. Just because I had been over the worst of that pain by the time

Rose was 10 days old, didn't mean that I would be so lucky the second time.

I was feeling more and more uncomfortable by the minute. I was confused, so very confused. I had left my baby so that I could be checked out, not so that some drill sergeant could grill me about whether I loved my baby. I started to feel panicked then. If she wasn't going to help me figure out why I was in so much pain then I needed to get back to Max. Mum would need to go and get Rose soon and I needed to be back in the room with my tiny boy. The woman was so intimidating but eventually, after maybe 15 minutes had passed, I told her that I really needed to get back to my son.

I didn't tell the horrible woman about the incontinence that I had been experiencing, and not just from my bladder. I remembered having to cross my legs to sneeze for a while after my first baby was born and I knew it was a common issue, but I had been losing control of my bowels and had been too embarrassed to tell my mum or anyone else. I had hoped that my trip to the midwife would give me some reassurance about my embarrassing new problem but I decided then to keep it to myself. There was no way I was going to let her make me feel even worse than what she already had.

At that point the woman asked if she could take a look at my stitches. She had read that I'd ended up with a fourth degree cut, meaning that I had been cut from the vagina, all the way down through my anal sphincter and into the mucous membrane that lines the rectum. I had no understanding of just

                    But baby, you're worth it!

how serious that was at the time, or that it was the likely cause of the pain and incontinence that I had been experiencing. All I knew at that moment was that I needed to get away from her and back to my little boy. She agreed to let me go but insisted that I book a home visit with her over the upcoming weekend.

I finally got away from her and back to the room where my tiny boy lay peacefully whilst Mum sat next to him, just quietly cooing and talking to him. Relief washed over me as I walked through those doors to see my mum quietly teaching Max to say Nan-nan, just as she had done with my little Rose.

As I walked around to face her, my mum asked if everything was okay, and I recounted what had happened. I explained that the woman had grilled me about my mental state for most of the time that I'd been in with her. I didn't tell Mum how she had demanded to book in a home visit though, even though the home visit nurse who had been to visit already, just a few days earlier, had been more than happy with everything. She had been happy to pass me onto the child and family health centre at Lane Cove. I'd seen those ladies often with Rose and had been looking forward to seeing them again the following week with my beautiful and handsome little boy.

To say that my mum was outraged would be an understatement. She was furious that the midwife had spent all that time making me feel even more distressed than I already did, instead of checking to see if I was okay physically. Mum wanted to go and put in a complaint. She had worked at that hospital for almost twenty years before retiring when her little brother, my beautiful Uncle Greg, was dying almost ten years earlier. She knew that patients were not supposed to be treated the way I just had been.

I was a terrified parent with a newborn baby in the hospital. I was in that fragile post-partum stage where not only were my hormones going haywire, but I was also in an unbelievable amount of pain. It had taken my mum and numerous doctors and nurses a fair bit of convincing to get me out of that room and down to see the midwife. I had gone down there hoping for some kind of reassurance, I figured that the woman would take a Quick Look at my stitches and deliver a verdict. Instead, I had walked out feeling so much worse than when I had walked in, if that was even possible.

I hadn't been back in the room for long when Mum left to go and pick up Rose. I was still waiting for the doctors to let me know what time we could go home. I was crossing everything in the hopes that we would be packed and ready to walk out of there by the time the girls got back, but unfortunately luck was not on my side. The doctors still hadn't managed to figure out what was wrong with Max and they weren't willing to let me take him home yet.

I was devastated by the news. I missed my little girl and I hated seeing my tiny baby with that needle in his hand. I hadn't been able to change his clothes in two days because I was so terrified of bumping the cannula and hurting my baby. I hadn't even been able to cradle my sweet baby in my arms for fear that it would hurt him.

　　　　　　　　　But baby, you're worth it!

Soon after Mum and Rose left to go home that second night, I was told by the funny doctor who'd been looking after us, that we would very likely be allowed to go home the following morning. I didn't want to get my hopes up, just in case but I was feeling hopeful. The doctor had also apologised about the commotion next door. It took me a moment to realise that he was talking about the child coughing, crying and screaming in the next room. It turned out that they should not have been in that room, so close to a newborn baby.

The child had been moved down to an isolation room at the other end of the hall as soon as he had come on shift that morning. That explained why I hadn't heard them for several hours. I couldn't help myself, I had asked what was wrong with the poor little thing. Although he wasn't allowed to tell me, the look on his face when I had asked if the child had whooping cough told me all I needed to know. I was grateful that I'd had a booster shot during my pregnancy, hoping it meant Max was protected too.

After another long and mostly sleepless night it really cheered me up to get a FaceTime call from Rose before she headed off to school the following day. She was excited about having her mum and baby home again finally. What was supposed to be a couple of hours at the hospital had turned into 3 days and I was over it. I was still in a lot of pain but I couldn't worry about that, I just wanted to get that horrid thing out of my little boy's hand.

I had been so terrified of bumping that cannula. I'd had enough of them myself over the years and so I knew how much it would have hurt. And I was an adult, I could at least understand why it hurt. It terrified me to think that my sweet little boy might feel scared if his hand was bumped and began to sting. I just wanted to be able to dress and cuddle my little boy again. I wanted to take him home where he was safe with his family.

Shortly before lunch on that third day we finally got the all clear to go home. I was relieved when the senior obstetrician declared Max to be perfectly healthy. His sweet little eye was looking completely fine again. As I had suspected from the start, there was no infection found. I was told that I would need to continue giving the oral antibiotics just in case. I was also told, ironically, that I would need to continue giving the very ointment that I had tried to buy in the first place.

Mum had been desperate to do a grocery shop and so I'd ordered her to go and do that after dropping Rose at school that morning, in case we had to wait around to be discharged. It worked perfectly in the end. By the time we'd finally made it to the car there was just enough time to stop and grab sushi for dinner before heading back for school pick-up.

I looked like absolute crap, far worse than I had looked 3 days earlier when Doctor Hottie had walked into that treatment room, but I couldn't have cared less. I left Max in the car with Mum, not wanting to take him near all of those germy kids. I waited patiently at the school gate, chatting to one of the mums who I had become close with as I waited for the bell to ring. I watched Rose walking from her classroom, chatting

   But baby, you're worth it!

happily with her friends as I waited for her to see me. Finally, she did and her face lit up.

I wasn't sure how much Rose had told her teacher but when Mrs. James saw me, she had mouthed "Are you okay?" With her fist clenched over her heart. Such a tiny gesture by that absolute saint of a woman but so very appreciated. I knew that she was looking out for my sweet girl when she was away from me. I had felt so anxious about everything while I'd been in hospital with Max but knowing that my mum and my daughter's beautiful teacher were both looking after her, had allowed me to focus on getting my little boy better and back home.

Chapter 5
Friday, 27th May, 2022

I t was such a relief to be home with my little family. Rose was as attentive as ever with her little Max. She was adamant that he was her baby and no one else's. I knew that it was common for an older sibling to feel resentment towards a new baby when they were taking up everyone's time but there were no such feelings from my big girl. That love that had washed over her the moment she'd met her baby brother was growing stronger every day. Especially after she hadn't been allowed to cuddle him while he had been in the hospital.

The first night back home was a bit of a rough one. Poor Max had been woken up so often while we were in the hospital that his sleep routine had gone completely out the window. He also started throwing up after his bottles. They were pink vomits that contained a combination of his milk and the pink antibiotic liquid that I'd been ordered to continue giving him for a week after we'd left the hospital. By the time we crawled out of bed on that Friday morning Rose was begging me to let her stay home from school. I was worried, though, because she had been off for 4 days the previous week after we'd welcomed our little boy.

But baby, you're worth it!

Rose was in such a crucial year at school. We'd both had Covid back in March, when I was about 32 weeks pregnant. We hadn't had a severe dose thankfully but it had still been a good week of man-flu like symptoms. I hadn't wanted to pass our germs on to anyone else and so I'd kept her home from school. I really didn't want her to miss any more time and so we agreed that I would drive her to school myself.

Somehow, we managed to leave the house a few minutes early. I hadn't driven in almost two weeks by that stage and I was nervous about driving a manual when I could hardly sit straight. I had been sitting on a pillow in the back of Mum's car whilst she drove everywhere, but I knew that my girl needed a bit of one-on-one time and so I ignored the pain in my groin and drove Rose to school without any trouble. We made good time and ended up grabbing her a hot chocolate from the bakery across the road.

As we walked back to the school an uneasy feeling washed over me. I really wished at that moment that I had just let Rose have one more day at home, but by that point we had walked across to the front gate. Rose's beautiful teacher, Mrs. James, was on gate duty and eagerly greeting us. She asked about how little Max was doing and was excited to see some more recent pictures of our sweet baby. The only ones she'd seen were the grainy pictures I'd printed from my phone from the first couple of days after he was born. Once I had shown Rose's teacher not less than 40 pictures, I wished them both a great day before heading back towards the car.

I drove home feeling happy. The horrible misadventure of our hospital stay was now behind us. I was ready to get on with life. As I drove home, I thought about the wonderful times that lay ahead. I wondered when my little boy would talk, what he would like to eat and what his first word would be. Rose's first word was Jing-Jing. My nephew Jonathan had been staying upstairs with Mum for the weekend and had just been picked up by my brother Nick, his dad. We'd had a wonderful weekend but as I was carrying Rose downstairs to get ready for bed, she had cried out Jonathan's name. Rose's baby version of it at least. Her next word was Nan-nan and then finally I got mama. I was secretly hoping that mama would be the first word this time.

Before I knew it, I was pulling into the driveway. I snapped myself back to reality as I carefully manoeuvred myself out of the car. I was in so much pain, and if I didn't know any better, I would have thought for sure that the pain was actually getting worse. But how was that possible? I could feel that the stitches were extensive, I wasn't surprised by that, considering how long it had taken the doctor to stitch me back up after Max was born. But it was day 11 and I was sure that I should have been feeling better by that point. I thought about the horrible midwife that had questioned my love for my little boy and I shuddered. I was terrified of that woman coming near my home. I had completely forgotten to tell Mum that she had demanded to visit me at home. I needed to tell her though, she was due to come the following day.

I pushed my thoughts aside. I was eager to get inside to my baby. I had never been away from him for so long before, and

But baby, you're worth it!

I'd been gone for 45 minutes at that point. I hurried in to see that Mum had just put the kettle on to warm up a bottle. Max was lying on the memory foam rug waiting to have his nappy changed. I headed straight over to say hello and kiss his sweet little forehead. Mum had been about to get down on the rug to change our boy's smelly bottom but I sat down, eager to sort him out myself, and to save Mum the hassle. My mum was very fit and mobile for a 71-year-old woman, but her knees weren't what they once were and she found it difficult to get herself back up off the ground.

Once Max was cleaned up and back in his snuggly little outfit, we settled onto the lounge to have a bottle and a cuddle. My poor baby was still on the antibiotics for his eye, which thankfully hadn't flared up again. I had been told to bring him straight back to the hospital immediately if the redness returned but his eye looked completely normal. The antibiotics were still making him vomit though and I was really starting to question why I was still giving them to him, given that his eye hadn't actually been infected after all. I was concerned that he must surely be losing weight, but I didn't want to risk his eye getting worse. I wasn't sure I could cope with seeing my baby back in the hospital, with another cannula in his tiny hand. So, I ignored my mother's instinct, once again, as I stroked his small back after he'd had his bottle. I encouraged him then to burp as I prayed silently that he wouldn't vomit too much.

After Max had been burped, and the inevitable pink milky vomit had been cleaned up, it was time for a sleep. I had started holding my little guy upright for half an hour after his bottle, in case he vomited again. Luckily, he slept soundly in that awkward upright position. Max may have had his routine turned upside down in that hospital room but he was still a pretty good sleeper. He slept for almost 3 hours. I laid him down carefully after that first half an hour, he'd been out like a light and hadn't even stirred. I even managed to doze off for an hour myself, despite the awkward position I was sitting in.

I messaged mum to let her know that Max was awake so she could come down stairs. Mum was concerned about the amount of pain I was in. She'd been in the operating theatre when I gave birth and so she'd seen the blood everywhere. My mum had been there when they had stitched me back up and so she knew how extensive my cut and tear had been from listening to the doctor and midwives. I was okay to do the basic tasks I needed to do, like changing and feeding my baby and cuddling him, but when he was awake, he hated being put down for more than a couple of minutes. Mum tried to insist that she could do my washing, vacuuming and the dishes but I wouldn't hear anything of the sort. I was happy for her to cuddle her sweet grandbaby while I looked after the house. I pushed the pain aside and got on with things. I had never been good at letting other people take care of me, my independence was something I had always been proud of, to a fault.

Half an hour later, I had tidied my kitchen considerably which made me feel a bit better. It was lunch time and so I had taken one of the meals I'd frozen a couple of weeks prior and popped it in the microwave before grabbing my phone to randomly check my main social media account. I had been a member of a

But baby, you're worth it!

local page called In the Cove, for many years. I loved being able to keep up with local news and events. During Covid they had run all sorts of competitions to get people in the community connected with their neighbours virtually. Rose and I had even won one of the competitions.

But as soon as I opened the page my heart just about exploded in my chest. There was an urgent news alert about a shooting nearby. I was confused because the news alert said that the shooting had happened in a nearby suburb, but that was impossible, that was the suburb where I'd dropped Rose just a few hours earlier. I wasn't familiar with the street names, it was something I'd always been terrible with, names of people and streets. The location was mentioned but it didn't sound familiar and so I thought it must have been a different part of the suburb. Before I had a chance to check the map on my phone the messages started, in the class chat and the app that the school used to communicate with parents. There was talk of the supermarket across the road, and then there were parents asking if one of the mums was okay. A person had been shot in a driveway just 2 doors up from her house. She'd been home and she'd heard the commotion and then the gunshots.

In an ever-increasing panic I checked my map: the incident had happened just a hundred metres from my little girl's classroom. I'd told Mum by that point. I was in a state. We turned the news on as I quickly grabbed my shoes and my coat. The school had sent a message to parents telling them not to come to the school, the children were safe, but they were not letting anyone

in or out. I couldn't stand there with my baby in such danger
— at that moment I needed to be near her — and so I kissed
my sweet boy ever so carefully on his sweet head, thanked my
mum and ran out the door.

I finally parked my car just a few metres from the school gate
about 15 minutes later. In my fragile state I had talked myself
into an absolute frenzy, convinced that I was going to be faced
with absolute mayhem but there was barely a soul around. The
school was on the corner of two streets. The shooting had
happened in the street opposite the main gates of the school
and so I had parked in the side street, right where I had parked
before walking Rose to school that very morning.

I hopped out of the car as quickly as I could. Immediately,
I noticed how quiet the school was. There were no children or
staff to be seen anywhere. The eerie silence was broken by the
sound of a man screaming. It took me a moment to register why
he was screaming. I looked in the direction that his aggression
was aimed at and suddenly I understood. There, standing across
the road on the footpath was a news cameraman with his video
camera set up on the tripod and trained on the school yard.
He was waiting for the children to come out, probably hoping
to get the money shot of terrified kids and parents scrambling
to get away. I was disgusted. If I wasn't in such a panic to get
to my daughter, I probably would have said a few choice words
myself. I agreed with the words spewing from the man's mouth.
Words like 'vulture' and 'opportunistic'. I could see the panic in
his eyes and I guessed that he had raced there like I had to pick
up his precious child, or children.

                                    But baby, you're worth it!

I walked along beside the fence but there was still no one in sight. The school had been sending constant updates via the app asking parents not to come to the school yet. It was almost 2pm by that time, the kids were due to be dismissed in a little over an hour and so I would just wait. I had called to check in on Mum and Max, everything was fine at home. Mum just wanted our precious girl safe at home as much as I did. I was thankful that Max and I hadn't still been at the hospital, the thought of not being able to rush to get my little girl right then was just about more than I could have coped with. I couldn't bear to think about how scared she must be. I was desperate to get to her.

I stood outside the school for a couple of minutes, one eye on the playground, the other on the two reporters that were starting to set up with their camera crews along the footpath that ran along next to the school. There were more parents showing up by the minute, and I could see that people were being questioned by the reporters. I didn't particularly want to walk past them, but I needed to get rid of some of my nervous energy.

I thought I might as well get some hot chips from the chicken shop over the road rather than just pacing back and forth. I started walking in the direction of the reporters and was instantly relieved when they intercepted a woman with a dog who was more than happy to speak with them. I had never seen her before, but that didn't mean much since Rose had only been at the school for a year-and-a-half. As I rounded the corner, I was shocked by what I saw.

There must have been 10 police cars opposite the front gates of the school. Some were blocking the road off while others were parked along the street. As I crossed the road I could see where the police tape had been used to rope off a driveway. I felt like I was looking at the filming of a tv show. I'd seen that many police officers once before. It was a few years earlier between Santa Monica and Venice beach, California. I was walking down to Venice to get a tattoo, when I stumbled upon a guy getting arrested by about 20 cops. It was such a strange thing to have witnessed. At first, I had thought that, surely, I'd seen a TV show being filmed but just hadn't realised. It was L.A though and so it wasn't a huge stretch to think that I could have been watching a real scene unfolding in front of me. Whatever that was, it was nowhere near as intimidating as seeing those police officers with their cars parked everywhere, just metres from the entrance of my child's school.

A few minutes later I was waiting for the two bags of chips I'd ordered when an alert came up on my phone from school. It was a message from the principal to say that the children could finally be collected. Parents were to come to the side entrance and children would be brought out as their parents arrived. I was ready to head straight out the door without the food I'd ordered but, thankfully, I was called to collect the chips just a moment later by the owner of the shop. He knew that I was a parent and wished me luck as I grabbed the paper bag and raced off.

I headed back towards the school with a sense of purpose. I could see the news crews were still setting things up but

I wasn't worried. I was on a mission to get my girl and get home. I passed the first reporter with no trouble at all. Just as I was sure I'd avoided the second reporter and her camera man she called me over. I kept walking, saying that I had to pick my child up but she insisted, stepping out onto the path from where she had been standing, almost behind a tree.

The woman introduced herself, there was no need though. I recognised her from one of the news programs I was familiar with. That woman asking if I was scared was the end of me. I had been so desperate to keep it together for Rose's sake but every ounce of bravado suddenly came crashing down. I told the woman that I couldn't talk to her, especially not on camera. She was so stunning, dressed in her pink suit with black heels. Such a contrast to my messy hair, maternity track pants and oversized Rabbitohs hoodie, with baby vomit on the sleeve that I hadn't even known about at the time.

I explained, as tears ran down my face, that my newborn baby had just been in hospital for the past 3 days. All I wanted was to get my older child from school and get back to the safety of our home. Thankfully, she moved aside and let me go without another word. As I continued towards the gate, I was thankful there were no other parents waiting.

The assistant principal immediately went to grab Rose. A minute later my girl appeared, walking from the main school building rather than from the direction of her own classroom. Rose looked like anyone who'd just been given an early mark on a Friday. She was happy to see me but she was confused, especially when she saw the state of me after I just about hugged the poor kid's brain out. As it turned out, the children hadn't been told what had happened.

I found out later that the police had called the school to advise that they should keep the children inside until they were given the all clear. The school knew that someone had been shot but they didn't know any more details than that. The kids were just about to break for lunch when the phone call came. The teachers had all been alerted within minutes to keep the children inside for lunch. Year 6, who were located in a separate building to the rest of the school had been walked quickly and quietly back to the main building. The kids had been scared despite not being told what was going on. They could never have imagined what had unfolded within view of their playground.

As we stood outside the school, I realised that there were a couple more news reporters in different stages of getting set up their equipment and 2 helicopters were circling above. I realised that they may have been there the whole time. I really wasn't sure. I started to feel panicked again, I needed to get my baby home to safety. I took my daughter's arm then and started to run. Rose didn't ask why, she just took my lead. I wasn't one to lose my mind for no reason. She knew in that moment that she needed to match my pace which, considering how much pain I was in, was not at all difficult.

We reached the car quickly. I ordered Rose to get in as I threw her bag in the boot, joining her in the front within a few seconds. Once our seatbelts were secured, we were off. I drove carefully

But baby, you're worth it!

home, aware of how distraught I was, the last thing I wanted was for us to have an accident. I talked to Rose, wanting to know that she was truly okay. I was grateful to the school for not telling the children what was happening. I told her the basics of what had happened as I drove, reassuring her that there was no further danger when she returned to school the following Monday, but not believing a word of what I was telling my daughter.

I was absolutely unraveling on the inside. First my little baby was kept in hospital for 3 days, for no good reason as it turned out. The midwife who I'd been convinced to talk to about my increasingly painful postpartum wounds had treated me like I was a bad mother and now my precious girl was in danger at school. It may not have been logical but as I arrived home, just 15 minutes after frantically jumping in the car, I wanted to take my family and barricade them inside, away from the dangerous world outside.

Chapter 6
Monday, 30th May, 2022

When we arrived home, I immediately told Mum about the midwife's plan to come to our home the following day. As I'd expected, she was furious. We had already booked an appointment with the family health clinic the following Wednesday. There really was no good reason for that woman to come into my home. The place was a mess, as you would expect with a newborn and an almost 12-year-old in residence. I was terrified that she would say that I wasn't fit to be a mother, that I wasn't fit to have my sweet little Max in particular.

My mum explained that I had every right to refuse the appointment. The way that woman had made me feel, whether she meant to or not, was not going to be conducive to a positive visit. I was nervous about talking to her but decided that I needed to try to cancel her visit. I dialled the number hoping that it would go to voicemail but, of course, no such luck. The woman answered on the second ring. I nervously explained who I was — and was more than a little bit annoyed when she couldn't remember me. That woman had judged me so harshly just a day earlier and she'd already forgotten about it. I realised then that it wasn't about me, that woman was not the same as the caring and beautiful midwives who'd looked after me when I was giving birth, and then afterwards in those first few days as I'd navigated having a newborn again after so long.

I was furious, the realisation gave me the strength to tell that woman, in no uncertain terms, that her visiting my home the following day did not suit me. I explained that I had other plans and so would not be available for her. The woman had realised who I was by that point. She tried frantically to figure out a time that would work, insisting that she needed to come. I waivered for a moment but as I glanced over at my mum, sitting with my children, I once again found the strength to stick to my guns. I had the phone on speaker, you see. And so I told her firmly that there was no good reason for her to visit me. I explained that I had an appointment on Wednesday and that everything was fine. That I loved my children and did not appreciate her suggestions to the contrary.

I had waited so long to have my tiny little boy. I could not have been more in love with him if I had tried. My children were the reason for everything I did, and I wasn't going to have some woman I'd spent less than half an hour with tell me or anyone else otherwise. I hadn't wanted to be in that hospital with my little baby but I hadn't been given a choice. I was a distraught mother with a sick baby, or at least I was led to believe that he was sick. I had come to see her because I was in a massive amount of pain and had been desperately hoping that she could help me. She'd done nothing of the sort. I was still in so much pain. I didn't need her shitty attitude adding to everything, especially after what we had been through that day.

I thanked her for her time and ended the call. I felt like I'd had a small win. A massive load had been lifted off my shoulders, knowing that I wasn't going to have that woman judging me again. While I was at it, I decided to quickly call the mobile number I'd been given for the hospital obstetrician on call. I had been asked to call the number if I had any questions or concerns about Max's eye. My poor little boy was still throwing up his bottles, he hadn't had any issues with vomiting until he was admitted to the hospital. I strongly believed that the antibiotics were to blame. The tests had shown no infection, the issue had been caused by a blocked tear duct, after all. I had been ordered to keep Max on the antibiotics for another week just as a precaution.

I'd read and heard so much about antibiotics being a problem when they were overused. I had once been refused a script for them when I had a raging throat infection, because the doctor, not my regular GP, believed that I should let my own immune system kick in to fight the infection. It made no sense to me that I was giving a tiny baby antibiotics when he didn't have an infection. And so, I was relieved, unlike the previous call, when a woman answered the phone. She took my details, and Max's name and date of birth, before asking me to call her Elizabeth.

As I explained the situation to her I was met with kindness and concern. Elizabeth asked questions about my baby, his eye,

But baby, you're worth it!

and just how he seemed in general. I was relieved also that she didn't ask about me. She quickly came to the conclusion that the antibiotics were doing more harm than good and agreed that they should be stopped immediately. I thanked her and, reassuring her that I would call if anything changed with Max, I ended the call. Immediately feeling better. I had been so stressed out about that woman's impending visit, and the likelihood the antibiotics that were actually making my baby sick. The news that someone had been shot near my daughter's school had been the tipping point.

The moment I ended the call with Elizabeth tears welled in my eyes. It had been a tough few days. I was sleep-deprived and in so much pain, but I was thankful to be there, in the safety of my home, with my mum and babies. I knew that we couldn't stay in there forever but for that moment we weren't going anywhere.

By Monday morning I had obsessively read every news article about the shooting. I needed to make sure it was safe to send Rose back there. Mum had been so worried that she'd tried to convince me we should start homeschooling immediately. As much as I wanted to keep my daughter safely at home, I knew that it wasn't the right thing to do for her. Covid had been such a shit storm. Not being able to connect with her friends, and then the bullying that had started again once face-to-face learning had returned. For the first time ever, Rose actually looked forward to walking through the school gates in the morning. And so, as scared as I was, I forced common sense to prevail. The shooting had been an isolated incident. There had never been anything like it in the suburb before. I wasn't sure that

I would ever feel safe about having my children out of my sight again, but I had to try and get over it, for my daughter's' sake.

And so, the school days came and went. I dreaded the hours that Rose would be away from me but I told myself over and over, like a mantra, that she was safe and there was nothing to worry about. My darling girl was okay. As each day passed, it was becoming more and more clear, however, that I was not. My stitches were starting to heal, and so it made no sense to me that the pain was becoming worse by the day.

But baby, you're worth it!

Chapter 7
Tuesday, 7th June, 2022

The days turned into weeks. Max had been to see both the community health nurse and our GP after that horrible hospital stay. Both women were appalled that my little boy had been placed on antibiotics. His eye was still playing up a bit but now that it was confirmed to be nothing more than the blocked tear duct, I was told to simply use the ointment for 3 days when it flared up. If it didn't stop flaring up and becoming weepy by the time Max was one, then I would need to take him to a specialist for a routine procedure to open the tear duct slightly. It sounded terrifying, but I was sure that things would sort themselves out before then.

Rose had gone back to school on the Monday after the shooting. Everything was back to normal as I'd known, at least logically, that it would be. The peaceful North Shore suburb was once more just that. But I was having trouble coping emotionally with her being away from home. I knew it wasn't logical at all, but I was having trouble shaking the growing sense of terror I was feeling whenever my children were out of my sight.

By the time Max was five weeks old, I was feeling more and more pain each day. I finally decided to listen to my instincts when I found what looked like a large piece of placenta on my maternity pad. It should've been enough of a sign that something was wrong, the fact that I was still wearing these huge uncomfortable maternity pads all those weeks after delivering my baby, but that horrible midwife had made it clear that I was just being silly. I didn't want to be a burden on the doctors and so I had tried to ignore the pain, sure that I was just being a hypochondriac.

As customary, I had booked a six-week checkup, long before I actually gave birth, to make sure that all was well and had gone back to normal after delivery. I'd been doing my pap smears and other female checks at a local women's health clinic for many years. I had had my six-week checkup done there after giving birth to Rose and so it made sense to me to book the check-up after my second baby as well. The appointment was only a week or so away, but I thought I should probably make an appointment to go in there ASAP. I called and they were able to get me in that afternoon. The receptionist confirmed that I should wrap and bag the piece of placenta and bring it along with me.

I arrived five minutes early, as I always did, regardless of the purpose of an appointment. I'm a firm believer in always arriving early, having been taught as a child that it was a courteous thing to do. I was met a few minutes later by a young female doctor that I hadn't met before, who asked me through to the room and invited me to take a seat. We talked for a few minutes as I explained to her some of my concerns. I explained about the pain and the bleeding, and the fact that I seemed to be getting

But baby, you're worth it!

worse. By this point, I had also developed a smell that I knew was not normal. I was so embarrassed, but I knew that I needed to tell her the full story.

She asked me to hop onto the bed so that she could examine me. She had a quick look and said that she suspected there may be a slight infection. She wasn't at all worried and suggested that a course of antibiotics would probably be necessary, just in case.

She then took a look at the piece of what I strongly believed was placenta. She was noncommittal after taking a very quick look and asked if she could throw it in the bin. I was shocked, I was under the impression that it would be sent off to a lab or something to check whether it was indeed placenta. Surely a piece this large, roughly the piece of my thumb, should not have been left behind. But she was the doctor. Not for the first time since giving birth, I decided to trust the doctor's opinion, rather than my own instinct.

I was advised that if the pain and bleeding were to continue, then I should organise to have an ultrasound. The doctor's suggestion was that I wait a week and then go for the scan if need be. I went straight to the pharmacy and picked up the antibiotics. Within a couple of days, I started to feel better. The pain had eased off significantly, and the odour had all but gone. I was so relieved. I am what you would call obsessive about hygiene. Some nasty guy, many moons ago, when I was just a teenager, had spread rumors about me, saying that I smelled bad.

Of course, he was just getting revenge because I didn't want to date him any longer. But at the time it really affected me and had turned me into even more of a clean freak than what I already was, so I knew there should not have been any kind of bad smell. It was something I had never experienced before, and I was so very relieved that the antibiotics were working and that everything was going to get better.

The effectiveness of the antibiotics was short-lived, however, and within two days of finishing the course that familiar pain and odour had begun to return. I hadn't thought much more about going for an ultrasound because I thought the antibiotics had done the trick, but at that point, I figured it was probably worth booking in to get things checked. A few days later, about 10 days after finding that piece of placenta, I arrived for my ultrasound.

The women were excited to see me. And to hear about little Max and see photographs of him. I had had my monthly scans during my pregnancy, because of my age, at the same clinic. I knew they were kind and thorough, and that if there was anything going on, I could trust them to figure out what was happening. As soon as the ultrasound began, it was extremely obvious that there was something still in my uterus. The mass was checked for vascularity, meaning that they were looking for blood flow, to figure out whether there were functioning pieces of placenta still inside me. I was relieved to hear there was none.

The results were inconclusive, but at least I knew I was not imagining that something was wrong. It's strange, but

But baby, you're worth it!

I actually felt a sense of relief. All those weeks I had known there was something going on that was not normal. I should have listened to my instincts. I should not have listened to that stupid midwife or any of the other people who had told me it was normal to be in so much pain, weeks after giving birth. After all, if there's one thing you learn after nine years of fertility treatments, it is what is and is not normal for your own body.

With the new information at hand, I organised a follow-up appointment with the women's health clinic. The results of the scan would be sent to them that afternoon and so I organised another emergency appointment for a couple of days later. By that point it was almost three weeks since my initial appointment.

Once again, I arrived for my appointment five minutes early. I was thankful that I had been booked with a doctor I was familiar with, she was a much more senior lady. I instantly felt relieved, I was sure she would be able to help me figure out what needed to happen next, to get me back to normal. By that point, I was a nervous wreck, I was so eager to get on with life, to be able to take my baby walking in his pram, go for drives and to be able to do all the things I had taken for granted with Rose. I was sure that once I was fixed up Max would magically start to like being out with me, that he would stop screaming whenever I took him out of the house.

As I sat down, the doctor brought up my records. I was shocked to learn that the doctor I had seen previously had not even recorded anything about the sizable piece of placenta that

I had passed and brought to the clinic with me a few weeks earlier. Once again, I was asked to lie on the table so the doctor could examine me.

I was shocked to learn that my cervix had actually dilated because of the extent of the infection, and because my body was trying to get rid of whatever was causing the infection. Once again, I had an immense amount of pain and foul-smelling discharge. The doctor confirmed that I did, indeed, once again, have a nasty infection. There was no mention of the retained products of conception, as they called it. The doctor was confident that, once again, a course of antibiotics would sort everything out. Once again, I was told to have another scan in a week's time.

Things were getting ridiculous. But I had, as mentioned previously, been attending the clinic for a number of years. It was a clinic that prided themselves on helping women with all kinds of sexual and reproductive health issues. If they weren't worried about the whole situation, then I reminded myself that I needed to stop being silly and just trust them.

So once again, I began the antibiotics. Once again, I started to feel a lot better within a couple of days. I had already booked a follow-up scan a week after the first and so when that day arrived, I headed up a bit early, even by my standards. I decided to treat myself to a doughnut and wandered around the shops for a while before my appointment, just as I had done so many times during my pregnancy, to make sure that Max was awake and cooperating during the scan.

                    But baby, you're worth it!

Finally, it was time to head across the road to the clinic for my scan. Once again, I was met by lovely ladies, who I'd become so familiar with over the past 10 months or so. I was relieved to see that the mass inside of me had decreased slightly. The woman who performed the scan couldn't tell either way whether it was actually placenta, just that there appeared to be less matter in my uterus than there had been on the previous scan. It made sense because I was definitely still bleeding, although it had turned more, as disgusting as this sounds, to a pussy type of consistency. At least it was coming out. Maybe things were finally sorting themselves out, after all.

I walked out of that clinic so relieved. By that time, my little Max was getting close to his next milestone, he was almost two months old. My tiny boy, who had brought so much joy into our lives. We already couldn't remember how we ever lived without the sweet little guy with his big blue eyes. The nasty red mark left on his face by the forceps was long gone and he was starting to get a few adorable wispy strands of golden-red hair. It was funny, even though my mum is a redhead, none of her three children had inherited her colouring, but both of my children had. I love it so much, that they look like their lovely nanna.

My relief was short lived. The day after the second scan, that now, all too familiar pain was back, as was the smell. I didn't need a doctor to tell me that the infection was back. But what now? Surely something could be done? I didn't know what to do, so I called the health clinic. The doctor wasn't available, so the receptionist assured me that she'd call me back that afternoon, I was satisfied by this, she'd know what to do next. We would make a plan. You see, I'm more than a little bit OCD, I mean, aren't we all? I thrive on plans, order. I don't like to wing it. I feel happy when there is order, I feel at ease when I know what the future will hold. We would get a plan in place, get this sorted once and for all, everything would be okay.

The hours passed, and no phone call came. Surely, I must have missed the doctor's call. The following morning, I once again called, once again left a message, and once again I heard nothing. Over the course of the next three days, I left five messages. Each time a little more desperate, until finally, on the third evening, I heard back. By that time, I was in so much pain, absolute agony. I could still barely sit down, which made no sense because I knew that the dozens of stitches I had needed during my labour had well and truly healed.

That was two months earlier, Max's birth. To say that the doctor was blasé was a gross understatement, she seemed genuinely annoyed. She demanded to know what I wanted her to do. She was the doctor, though. I was confused, I was relying on her to help me. After all, shouldn't she know what to do? I burst into tears because I was in so much pain. Finally, she agreed to refer me back to the hospital where I'd given birth. She promised to send an urgent referral on to the clinic, the same clinic I'd become familiar with over the course of my pregnancy. The hospital would call me to book me in urgently, she promised. She would send the referral too, for my own records. It was Friday 1st July.

But baby, you're worth it!

Rose was on her mid-year break from school so it was hard to keep track of exactly what day it was. Anyone with school-aged kids would know what I mean. School holidays are a huge blur, the days run into each other, especially in winter, when it's too cold and wet to play outside. Kids eat like horses. Well-stocked pantries everywhere were starting to resemble something straight out of Old Mother Hubbard's kitchen. It always puzzled me how sitting around and watching TV all day can make children so hungry! Monday came and went. Why hadn't the hospital called?

First thing Tuesday I was on the phone, feeling pretty annoyed that no one had bothered to call me the day before. I'd seen the referral by that point, it had "urgent" scrawled across the page in large capital letters. Surely, they should have been in touch as soon as they'd received it, to book me in as soon as they could. But I was polite when an older lady answered the phone — you catch more bees with honey than vinegar, after all. An old boss of mine had reminded us of this fact often enough when dealing with difficult clients, and it was so true. I explained the situation, and she was apologetic, she must have missed the referral. She placed me on hold so that she could find it. I hummed along to Taylor Swift's song, *The Man*, for a minute or two and before I knew it, she was back.

The lady was apologetic. She'd had a good look and nothing had been sent. The doctor hadn't bothered to send it. I was absolutely gob-smacked. It was shocking. I was reeling, but the woman on the other end of the phone was so kind and reassuring that she instantly made me feel better. I had an appointment booked in for the following Thursday morning. In a few days I was going to be all fixed up. I was going to be back to normal and I couldn't wait.

I hadn't been able to exercise since I was six weeks pregnant. I'd had a huge bleed just after exercising. I had been sure that I was once again miscarrying, but it had turned out to be a large blood clot called a sub-chronic haematoma. The clot had cleared and everything had been fine with my pregnancy after that. I hadn't exercised again though, just in case.

I had always loved walking, especially around the waterfront just minutes from home. I would walk along, dreaming about owning one of the waterfront mansions down in Longueville. Somehow, I was determined to make it a reality one day. My plan had always been to ease back into my walking once Max was a few weeks old, just as I had done with Rose. But I had been in so much pain, I could barely sit even now. I was still finding it hard to drive and it took everything I had to walk a few metres. I had never, at that point, held my little boy without being in a significant amount of pain. I couldn't wait for Thursday to arrive.

Chapter 8
Thursday, 7th July, 2022

Thursday morning finally rolled around, and I was eager to get things sorted out. The afternoon before I had tried to take a nap. The kids were happily hanging out with my mum. Max was going through his first sleep regression and I was exhausted, a couple of hours sleep would be absolutely wonderful, so in I went. I hopped into bed with my lovely electric blanket on high, it was so toasty, I lay in bed ready to drift off when, all of a sudden, the most immense pain ripped through me. I'd been living on painkillers on and off for weeks but I hadn't experienced anything quite like this before.

It fell like my uterus was going to fall out. There was no chance I'd be able to fall asleep with that pain radiating through my pelvis. I slowly maneuvered myself out of bed and walked back out to the loungeroom where Rose was playing with little Max on the memory foam rug I'd purchased a few weeks earlier. They were having a lovely time with rattles and teddy bears while Mum watched and talked to them both from the lounge. The girls were confused, why wasn't I in bed, they asked. But I couldn't sleep. I told Mum about the pain and she wanted me to go the hospital, but there was no point.

I was so tired, what was the point of sitting in the emergency department for 10 hours? I needed to be at home. I needed to protect my babies from the dangerous world. I'd always been such a happy-go-lucky person. I'd always had OCD and Covid definitely hadn't helped things, of course. My hands were always so washed or sanitised I could probably serve you a meal with my bare hands with no trouble at all. They would be cleaner than a plate straight from your dishwasher.

But I had become more and more compulsive about cleanliness and my children's safety over those last couple of months. Max's bottles had to be shaken exactly 50 times. I recorded each bottle on a notepad to make sure he was getting enough nutrients each day, convinced that he was going to starve because of his reflux and vomiting. I had become obsessed with his safety, so much so that I had become almost terrified to take him out of the house. If I cleaned up a dirty nappy, I would spend several minutes afterwards scrubbing my hands and fingernails to make sure that I didn't contaminate him, or anything of his that I touched.

I was convinced that he would die if I didn't do all those things. I was becoming more and more convinced that the world was out to get me. I would worry about Rose being at school where I couldn't take care of her after the shooting, convinced that it was going to happen again, but that she would be injured, or worse, the next time. None of it was rational, but I just couldn't shake the feeling of impending doom that constantly seemed to followed me, like one of those mini rain clouds that hover over a cartoon characters head.

But baby, you're worth it!

A few weeks earlier I'd had a lunch to attend at a nearby pub. I don't remember what the occasion was, but I was feeling pretty good that day so decided to brave it and take little Max with me. There was a woman in attendance that I barely knew. She seemed to have this idea that she had a right to touch my baby and she snatched him from me because she wanted to have a cuddle. It caused me so much anxiety that I ended up bursting into tears and screaming for my mum.

Mum had come along, as she did whenever I left the house with Max. She was at the bar, getting us both a drink. She didn't hear me scream but returned after a couple of minutes to see me in a panicked state. My best friends still hadn't met my sweet little boy, and there was some woman I barely knew snatching him with an absolute and outright sense of entitlement. I was beside myself for days afterwards.

I had become something I didn't recognise. I was convinced that the doctors were purposely not helping me. I was sure they wanted me to suffer, just like that horrible midwife I'd seen when Max was in hospital for his eye. I was convinced I wasn't good enough to be his mother and that woman snatching my precious baby just added to my feelings. From that day onward, whenever I was around people who wanted to touch my baby, or try to hold him, other than my closest family and friends, I would wear him in the carrier. Nobody could get him that way. I knew in moments of clarity that I was being ridiculous, but I was still too scared to share my fears. I didn't want to risk having someone tell me that I wasn't fit to look after my babies. I had waited such a long time to finally have my sweet little boy and I was terrified that people would think I was ungrateful if I dared to complain about the way I was feeling.

But the next morning, finally, I was going to get better. As I sat waiting to be called in to see a doctor, I looked around me at all of the hopeful, pregnant women. I genuinely hoped they would all have an easy time with their labour, that nobody would suffer the way I had. I felt self-indulgent, after all, I'd been told that I was being dramatic all those weeks ago when I had gone to that woman about the pain I was in. She had been so dismissive, and so I had continued to convince myself, over and over, that I was just being dramatic and imagining all of my issues. Even people I had asked, work colleagues and others, had told me that second babies took longer to recover from.

I was called in after waiting for about half an hour, I was quite familiar with the routine by that stage. I was asked to sit in a chair next to the doctor's desk. A female doctor came and sat down at the desk and asked me what had been happening. I explained everything that had happened over the past couple of months and she had the grace to look horrified. She apologised profusely, which made me feel a bit better. I still wasn't convinced that they were going to help me at the hospital, but I didn't know where else to go. As usual, the doctor asked me to get myself ready and pop up on the table, saying she would knock before entering the room to come and examine me. By this point, I had no dignity. So many doctors, midwives, and radiographers had examined me, but I guess that's normal for any woman who has been through childbirth.

But baby, you're worth it!

Much to my relief, the lady doctor was absolutely appalled by what she saw. My cervix was at least a centimetre dilated, and she could easily see that something was oozing out. After only a minute or so, she excused herself, saying she needed to go and get one of her colleagues to discuss things with. Over and over, she apologised. She couldn't believe that I had been left in such a state for so many weeks. The doctor covered my lower half with a sheet when she excused herself.

Not a minute later, a midwife tapped on the door. She had been asked to come in and check in with me. I hadn't even realised that I was sobbing. I was just so relieved that finally somebody believed me, finally someone agreed there was nothing normal about what I was experiencing. The lovely midwife had been sent in to reassure me and look after me while I waited for the doctors to come back into the room. She promised that they would not let me suffer any longer, they would get me fixed up and back to my babies.

A few minutes later, the original doctor walked in with a more senior obstetrician, both women. The doctors wanted to know if it was okay to take another look, sure, I was more than happy for them to help me, relieved that finally someone wanted to. Both doctors tutted, they were outraged on my behalf that I had been left for so long, that I had been allowed to get to that point. There was nothing normal about being dilated so many weeks after my son was born. There was nothing normal about that smell, or the pain I had been experiencing. They were furious about the way I had been dismissed by those other doctors.

Both women promised as they finished up that they would get things sorted out. There was a sense of urgency, I could tell the doctors were concerned. As the original doctor walked towards the door, she asked me to get dressed and to take a seat. She needed to make some calls but would be back shortly. I checked in with Mum. Everyone was fine. Nick had been calling for updates, he and Skye sent their love, just get myself sorted, Mum said. Everyone will be fine.

I didn't know what I would do without my mum. She was the best human being I'd ever known. She'd raised my brothers and I by herself from the time I was 14. And even before that she'd been the one who had always done everything for us. She'd worked three jobs to make sure we had everything we needed, and so much more. I didn't understand until I was well and truly an adult, just how much she had gone without, how much she had sacrificed in order to give us so much. She loved and cared about us enough to say no.

I had been such an angel child until I hit my mid-teens, but she never wavered, like so many parents seemed to do when the challenges of raising teens became too much. She was there for me, always. I soon grew out of that stage and into a woman, and as each year has passed, I had grown to appreciate her more and more, especially once I became a mother myself.

My mum, Margaret, the little 5'3" lady with the fiery copper hair that my beautiful babies had both inherited. She would give you her last $5, the shirt off her back and the food off her plate

But baby, you're worth it!

without you ever needing to ask. Always looking after others before herself, whether it was her children, grandchildren, animals or even other people's children. She would never dream of asking for anything in return, I knew that my babies were safe with their nanna. It was time for me to focus, just for a few moments, on myself.

The door opening brought me back from my train of thought about Mum and my babies. As I looked away from my phone I heard, and then saw, the two doctors as they entered the room. They were talking about another obstetrician, they had made some calls. I needed surgery as soon as possible, they believed that I had retained products of conception, in other words, yes, they believed there was still some of Max's placenta inside of me. They believed that my body was trying, unsuccessfully, to rid itself of whatever had been left inside.

One thing that they were certain about was that I had a nasty infection and I needed it sorted out urgently. If left much longer they believed the infection could become fatal. They had contacted a few obstetricians, and it turned out that one had a place that afternoon on his list. There was another option, they could give me another, much stronger course of antibiotics and get me into a public hospital an hour away, but that would take a week. They strongly advised I take the spot that afternoon because I needed the placenta removed urgently. It wasn't ideal that there would be a cost. I would have to go to a different hospital nearby to have the procedure, but it really couldn't be left any longer.

I had two hours to be at the other hospital. So, I headed home. I had so much to do. Bottles needed to be made, food prepared for Rose. By the time I got home it was 1pm. I had left the house at 9am that morning, it was the longest I had ever been away from my little boy. I was terrified that I would end up forced to stay in hospital for the night. I'd been told that I should be fine to go home once the anesthetic had worn off after the operation but if there were any issues then I could find myself in overnight.

I hated the thought of being away from my babies for a whole night but I knew that I needed to get better. I needed to be the best I could for my babies. I was becoming more obsessive and paranoid about everything. Silly things, I know that now, but I wasn't well, those couple of months had taken their toll on my mental health as well as my physical health.

Rose and Max were absolutely the loves of my life, but I wasn't enjoying them if I was completely honest. Max cried a lot, it had been painful to hold him from the day after he was born, once that glorious spinal block had worn off. Rose was 12, and overnight she'd suddenly grown up so much. She was such a good kid, she was well behaved, polite, I'd always been so proud of her but lately I'd found myself constantly snapping at her. I didn't mean to, I was just in so much pain, I didn't know that she was scared. My poor girl had been lying awake at night crying, and wondering if her mummy was going to go back to normal soon. In a few hours things were going to change, though. I was going to be me again. I was going to be her happy and fun mum again, and for that I could not wait.

I made my way to the hospital. I had ordered a ride share again. Max hated the car and so it was better to leave Mum at home with the kids, in the safety of our home. I'd travelled overseas many times by myself so a short trip to the hospital was no big deal. I arrived with about 15 minutes to spare and was ushered through to a small room. Within a few minutes I was changed into a hospital gown. It was the middle of winter and even in that big, air-conditioned hospital, it was cold.

A nurse brought me a heated blanket to help warm me up and it was pure heaven. For the next half an hour or so I played on my phone, checking in with Mum. We were supposed to be heading to Florida for our next Disney trip in just eight weeks and my younger niece, Ally, needed her passport renewed so we needed to chase Michael to get that sorted.

Halfway through messaging my friend Tina with a progress report a friendly young guy came in and announced that he would be wheeling me through to the operating theatre. The doctor was ready for me and so off we went. A nurse walked with us and it was quite an entertaining ride, my driver turned the bed into a race car. For a few minutes I smiled and laughed. That guy was surely wasting this wonderful talent, but then maybe he wasn't. Maybe he was doing exactly what he should be, taking scared, nervous people in a moment when they're feeling so vulnerable and making them smile and laugh. For a few moments he made me forget about everything else that was going on in my life. I was so very grateful for the distraction.

Max hadn't been sleeping well over the past couple of weeks and so I was looking forward to being — how do I say this? — knocked out! I was exhausted, both physically and mentally. I couldn't wait for a nice deep sleep, even if it was only for half an hour. I was wheeled into the anesthetic bay and almost immediately met by the obstetrician. He was a pleasant man in his early 50s. He explained that he would be doing a D&C. I was familiar enough with the procedure. I'd had to have them done after a couple of my miscarriages, both before and after Rose was born. The infection would be treated with intravenous antibiotics, and I should have no further issues once the operation had been completed. I was told to expect some light bleeding for a week or two but then everything would be back to normal.

The anesthetist came out then, it was time to get the show on the road. A cannula was inserted expertly, it stung a little, but I didn't care. It was nothing compared with the pain I'd endured over those past couple of months. I was wheeled into theatre and had to scoot onto the operating table, it was a lot easier to maneuver myself from one to the other than it had been last time, just after I had given birth. I had already lost the 18kg I'd gained while I was pregnant with Max. Most of the weight had been baby related and the rest had dropped off without any effort. With everything going on I hadn't had time to prioritise food, not for myself anyway. Within a couple of minutes, I was counting down from 10. I got as far as 8, 7.... I felt so drowsy.

But baby, you're worth it!

Chapter 9

Thursday, 7th July, 2022 - Continued

It's so warm. That was my first thought as I woke up. The nurses had placed another heated blanket on me. It felt wonderful. As I came to, I began to feel quite sick but before I knew it something had been put into the cannula and I instantly felt better. I hadn't been awake for long when the obstetrician who'd performed the surgery came over to see me. I was in recovery and would stay there until I left. There had been several pieces of placenta left inside, but he had removed everything and was confident that the two courses of intravenous antibiotics he had given me, the second of which was still running on a drip, would sort out the infection.

Once again, I was told to expect some bleeding and tenderness for a week or so. It shouldn't be anything like what I had experienced over the last nine weeks though. I was so relieved. I was excited to get home to my babies, and to get back to being myself. There would be a follow-up appointment in a few weeks. Someone from his rooms would be in touch the following week.

I soon had my belongings. The first thing I did was check in with Mum. It was getting late, so I messaged rather than calling to make sure I didn't wake Max if he was having a nap. Tina would be coming to collect me and drop me at home so I messaged her next, to let her know I'd be ready soon. By that point the drip with the antibiotics had finished and a nurse had removed the cannula. I hated those things and was happy to have had it taken out, to be able to move my hand again. I knew I would need to be careful not to bump my hand for a couple of days but it was, once again, a small price to pay.

After another hour or so I was starting to get annoyed. No one had been able to tell me when I would be allowed to leave. Tina had already had to move her plans for the evening around, as she had expected to pick me up by 5pm. Finally, I was free to leave just before 7pm and by the time I had made my way down to the front doors my wonderful friend was already there waiting for me.

Fifteen minutes later I had been carefully installed on the lounge at home, Mum and Tina fussing over me as Rose played with little Max. My niece, Ally, was there enjoying my funny little boy as well, all dressed up in his Rabbitohs onesie. Ally usually spent a few days with us during the school holidays and my brother Michael had dropped her off the day before. It was lovely to be fussed over, but mostly I was thrilled to be home. I was excited about having a few more weeks off to heal and to finally really enjoy my sweet baby before I started work again.

But baby, you're worth it!

Work had been absolutely wonderful and so supportive of the whole crazy mess. I had only been in the job for a little over three months when Max was born. I had been laid off from my previous job after several years, just a few months into my pregnancy, but I had been lucky enough to secure a new job with a wonderful company. I was supposed to return to work when my new baby was only a few weeks old. I was confident that everything would be fine. I would be working remotely and so would be able to work around my little guy's schedule and Mum would mind him whilst I was at my desk working.

I worked right up until the Wednesday before I gave birth, meaning that I had five days to get the place completely ready, and also to rest. When I was pregnant with Rose, I'd read some ridiculous article that said babies sleep as much on the outside as they do on the inside, so those last few weeks when I had started my maternity leave before I was due with her, I shopped, and socialised up a storm. My baby was a good sleeper so we'd just chill out and nap lots when she arrived. Well, I wasn't that ignorant, or perhaps gullible second time around. I'm not sure which one is worse? Either way, I knew better. Rose had been a terrible sleeper, for the first six weeks I averaged about two hours a night.

I had logged in to start back at work several weeks earlier when Max was less than three weeks old. It had only taken half a day for me to realise that it wasn't going to work. Of course, in hindsight, it was only days before the infection started to become apparent. I could never have imagined then what was about to unfold. All I knew was that I could not work like that.

I spoke to my manager. He was a lovely young guy, who'd only been with the company for a couple of months when I had started back in January. He didn't have any children, but he was so supportive and I was given another month off. I was asked to do a few hours once a week to check in and just keep my sales campaigns running. By the time the month was coming to an end, I was running back and forth trying to sort out the infection, and once again work had been so understanding. They were willing to extend my leave. I should mention too that they were actually giving me paid leave, despite having only worked for them for a few minutes in the scheme of things.

My big boss, who was based offshore, did have a wife and children. He was sympathetic and he wanted to look after me, the way he would hope that his wife would be looked after had she ever found herself in such a horrible situation.

Once I'd had the operation, I had another two weeks off before I was due back at work. Finally, I would have a bit of quality time with my babies before I was glued to my desk all day. It hadn't exactly been a relaxing way to spend my extended leave, but at least I'd been able to spend more time with Max than I had originally anticipated, and for that I was grateful.

I was home, all fixed up and returned to my beautiful little family. Everything was going to be okay. I was sure of it.

     But baby, you're worth it!

Chapter 10
Tuesday, 16th August, 2022

The weather was colder than I could ever remember experiencing in Sydney. Winters here certainly were not warm, whether you lived near the ocean or out west, and it was normal to need jumpers and coats in the morning and afternoon. Goodness knows, I had spent many a work commute over the years into the city with gloves, scarf and a beanie, the scarf wrapped around my face. That winter was different though. Normally the sun would be quite warm if you stood outside for a few minutes. Not that winter, though. I dreaded giving Max a bath, he hated the cold and our cosy granny flat was only heated by a small oil heater.

We didn't have any central heating; we'd never needed it before. Rose and I had our big fluffy oversized hoodies. We'd even kept Rose's smaller one for when our little Max was old enough to wear it. But it was so cold that even those hoodies weren't enough to keep us warm. Nothing had worked to keep us warm and so I was absolutely counting the days until the warmer weather came. I was also counting the days until I would start to feel completely better after the operation. The terrible pain I had experienced after giving birth and once the infection had started were gone, but something still didn't seem right. The pain had been replaced with a strange heaviness in my stomach and in my groin. Once again, I couldn't remember any of those things after Rose was born.

Ten days had passed, and I was due back at work in just a few days. Max was almost three months old and he was developing the funniest and sweetest personality. The big smiles and the funniest little chuckling had well and truly started. Rose was absolutely the funniest and most exciting person he had ever met. She was getting smiles for a good month before I finally got my first one. The ugly painting that I'd been given years ago and that sat on the wall next to his changing mat, in the lounge-room, was also getting smiles weeks before I was.

A boyfriend had given it to me years before and I had always intended to donate it or throw it out. The day I brought Rose home from the hospital, she was having a cuddle with Mum on the lounge when suddenly she caught sight of the big bold monstrosity behind her, and she was in love. Rose had been absolutely obsessed with that painting and now Max was too. I was destined to keep the horrid thing forever.

Baby Max was thriving. He was growing perfectly despite the ongoing reflux, but for some reason I was still bleeding. I'd had the procedure to remove the retained placenta and treat the infection almost two weeks before and was not at all ready to get back to work. So off I went to the GP. She'd been my doctor for 30 years or so. She'd seen me through bouts of cold and flu, miscarriages and all manner

But baby, you're worth it!

of other ailments over the years. My family doctor had been seeing Rose since she was a week old and the moment that I walked into her room she was concerned; I knew that I wasn't looking well.

My usual bronzed face, whether from the sun or a liberal dusting of bronzing powder, had been replaced by an almost grey pallor, but I hadn't expected her reaction. She immediately reached out and held my arm as I walked into her room to help me to one of the seats across from her desk. The doctor agreed that I should not be feeling so unwell still. The continued bleeding at that point was not normal either. In her opinion, there was no way I should be returning to work the following week. A note was quickly drafted giving me another five weeks off to finish recovering. The doctor also ran some blood tests that day to try and figure out if there was anything sinister going on — but after the tests came back without any issues I was cautioned that the slow recovery time was likely related to my age and told to rest.

Work were once again so very understanding. However, they were not going to be able to pay me for any more time off. I completely understood. I'd only been with the company for seven months, and I'd been on paid leave for the past three. Having another five weeks meant I could really focus on getting better. I knew that my mental health had taken an absolute battering over the past few months, so I would have a bit more time to get that sorted as well. I'd had some mental health struggles in the past, including when Rose was a baby. I had ended up on antidepressants because of the PTSD that resulted from the traumatic birth and so I knew things would get better soon, just as they had last time.

I was excited about exercising again too, at least walking. That terrifying day early in my pregnancy, the last time I'd gone walking, had been in September 2021, almost a year earlier. Never in my life had I gone a year without exercising and I was so keen to pull on my fluorescent running tights and one of my cheesy Walmart t-shirts and get moving. Soon, I'd be able to get out in the fresh crisp air and do something about my not-so-washboard tummy.

Although I'd lost all the baby weight, and even an extra few kilograms, the aftermath of having had polyhydramnios, a condition where baby is surrounded by too much amniotic fluid, had left its mark. Thankfully, there were no health implications for Max from the extra fluid, as can often be the case. The only issue it had caused was to my poor old belly. The time had definitely come to retire my bikinis, not that I'd worn one of those in years, even though I had kept a number of them, just in case.

Walking wouldn't get me the washboard abs that I'd sported for a few months in my late 20s, the result of a fitness craze that had ended in a broken foot. Walking was good for the soul though, and it would at least help, if only slightly, to turn my tummy frown upside down.

Finally, about three-and-a-half weeks after my hospital visit the bleeding was gone. It was mid-August and Max was three months

But baby, you're worth it!

old. Time is a funny thing when you have a new baby. Those sleepless nights drag on. The days can become monotonous when you're trying to establish routines. At the same time, your baby grows, they grow out of your favourite little outfits. You want time to slow down. You want them to reach milestones and do exciting things, but you want them to stay little. It's such a strange time.

The pain from that nasty infection was finally gone. It had been replaced, though, by a strange tenderness in my lower stomach and heaviness in my groin. I didn't remember anything like it with Rose. Maybe it was that dreaded first period post baby, getting ready to arrive with a vengeance. That must be it, surely? There was no other sensible explanation.

I pushed the strange feeling in my tummy and tenderness aside, just as I had done with the pain from the retained placenta and infection. I wasn't actually in pain as such, and I had so much lost time to make up for. It was time to get on with my life and start enjoying my children again. I was going to get back to smashing my sales targets at work, just as I had done, quarter after quarter at my last company. Even more importantly, it was time to think about the birthday that Rose had almost completely missed out on celebrating back in late June. Life was going to be good again. All I had to do was ignore that annoying nagging feeling, telling me that something was still not okay.

Chapter 11
Friday, 2nd September, 2022

Finally, Rose was going to get the birthday party I'd promised her. Her birthday had been back in late-June, which was right around the time my issues were starting to really become apparent. Not only had she ended up missing out on the traditional family dinner that the birthday person was always celebrated with, but my sweet girl also missed out on the party I'd promised her. It was her last year of primary school; she wasn't going to the same high school as any of her friends from her current school and so I'd said she could have a special party.

After going back and forth for a couple of days we had decided that Rose would have an ice-skating party and so we were excited to organise everything. I decided to hold the party early in the morning so Max would sleep for most of the time that we were out. It still absolutely filled me with dread when I had to leave home for anything more than school pick-up or a quick trip to the shops to get groceries, even then I would usually do click and collect, rather than wasting time wandering the aisles. Anything longer and I'd be riddled with anxiety. The party was booked on Sunday, 4th September at 9am. We would skate for 2 hours then head up to the food court for fries and sundaes before heading back to the ice rink foyer for kids to be picked up at 12.

I was due back at work the following Monday. I was still having the strange tenderness in my tummy, which had actually become distended as well. I looked like I had eaten a couple of hamburgers, but I knew that I hadn't put on weight because according to the scales I was down to 62 kilograms, more than a stone lighter than I had been when I first became pregnant with Max. The heaviness in my groin was still there as well. It had once again become extremely difficult to sit down.

It had also become almost impossible to drive my beloved car, a late model Rav 4 that I'd bought a year earlier and so, with a heavy heart, I decided to sell it. I had loved driving my little manual before giving birth to Max but I was in so much pain that driving it was no longer enjoyable. I was also worried about the financial side of things. I hadn't earned any commission in months and so Mum and I agreed that it made the most sense to sell my car and keep her seven-seater. The day finally approached, in the week leading up to the party, that the car was going to a new family and as it turned out the timing was perfect. I was just about to learn about the decision being made by my company — that their Australian operations were going to close down. I hadn't yet returned from my leave but I knew that when I did, just a few days later, I too would be losing my job.

I had heard whispers a few weeks earlier that this may be coming so I was already on the hunt for a new job. Despite all the madness of those past few months, I had always intended to return to my job once I was better but I couldn't risk not having a job to go back to. I had some savings and the small amount of income from our investment property, but I was determined not to dig into that money any more than I already had.

I was relieved that the car had been sold before I found out about my job. I knew that I would have had to take a lower offer. I was pretty disgusted by some of the ridiculous offers that people were sending me but at least I had sold the car for a reasonable price to a decent and honest family. I knew they would take care of her, just as I had.

I had a final interview lined up the following week. My prospective new boss would be flying to Sydney from Melbourne just to interview me face-to-face. I was pretty sure I had the job in the bag, so at least losing my current job wouldn't be a complete disaster.

In the few days leading up to the party, we had fun making lolly bags. I knew I would probably be losing my job the following week, but I was confident I would be offered the new role after my interview a couple of days later. It was actually my dream job. I would be working as a Partner Engagement Consultant for an Australian company. I was keen to work for an Aussie company for a few years, I didn't want to work for a US company and go gallivanting off to America while Max was so little.

I had really loved to travel for work. Mum and Rose always had a lovely time when I was away. They would go to the park or the

   But baby, you're worth it!

beach for picnics and they had even started a tradition where they would go to a local sushi restaurant in Lane Cove for a date night whenever I was overseas.

I was never gone for more than a week and had always returned with a suitcase full of gifts for my girls. But I hadn't started travelling until Rose was three, and even then, it had been heart-wrenching leaving her. I had only done it so that I could get ahead in my career and earn enough money to give my daughter everything she could ever want or need. But there was no way I was leaving my little baby any time soon, so everything was going to work out beautifully.

Finally, it was the Friday before Rose's party. It was also my niece Brittany's birthday. Brittany was just starting her HSC so it was a low-key celebration, just some takeaway pizza and donuts at home. The following year would be her 18th, and that was going to be a big party. We had already booked the function room at my friend's restaurant, Attimo, for the celebration. That weekend she was keen to catch up with friends. So, as it turned out, I would be wrangling the girls by myself at the ice rink but I reminded myself that it was only for a couple of hours. And anyway, they were 11- and 12-year -olds, not little 5-year-olds. Rose really deserved to have a morning that was just all about her, and I was sure it would be a piece of cake.

Sometime after the birthday celebrations had concluded for Brittany, I was getting everyone ready for bed, Max had just fallen asleep in his bassinet next to my bed. Rose was finishing her Japanese practice before she brushed her teeth for the night. We only have one bathroom and Rose is a champion at brushing those pearly whites, especially since the acquisition of her electric toothbrush a few months earlier. So, I popped in to use the loo quickly first.

It had been five weeks or so since I'd had the operation to remove the retained placenta, or 'products of conception' as the doctors had called it. The tenderness and inability to sit comfortably had definitely not gone away, and I wasn't sure if I was imagining it, but it actually seemed to be getting worse again. I don't know what made me check then, at that very moment, but I did. I checked gently to see if anything seemed off. Straightaway, I knew what was going on. I was horrified. I couldn't believe it at first, so I checked again. I wasn't imagining it though. My Cervix was almost falling out of my body.

Suddenly the tenderness and discomfort when sitting all made sense. Holy shit! I tried not to panic, it wasn't actually falling out, but it certainly was not where it should be. Any woman who had been through years of fertility treatments, and even those who hadn't, by my age should know their bodies well enough to know where everything goes. But how on earth had it happened? Max was almost 4 months old. Surely, if it had been caused by the infection it would have happened earlier?

My heart sank and a cold chill ran down my leg. Not my spine as you often hear about in movies, but my leg, of all the strange places. Could it have happened as a result of the forceps? My mind was going back over everything I had read in the months since having Max. Forceps were destructive things. I'd read all

But baby, you're worth it!

sorts of horror stories about women who had been severely injured, and babies who'd been left brain damaged or even killed, and everything in between, because of the use of forceps.

Something like a quarter of forceps deliveries ended with injuries of varying degrees — and that was just some of the things I had read. I was now sure that the forceps, and significant cutting and tearing, were the cause of the incontinence I had been suffering from since my baby had arrived in mid-May.

I was wearing maternity pads still, all those months on, because not only did I still have issues with wetting myself, but I was still losing control of my bowels. From what I had read that too was a common issue that occurred after a forceps delivery. I had got to the point where I was dropping anti-diarrhea tablets daily and eating as little as possible to try and minimise the embarrassing new issue that had developed since Max was born. I wasn't able to exercise still and yet I was losing more and more weight by the week because I had become almost paranoid about eating, in case I had an accident when I was out of the house.

I remembered the ice-skating party. I'd promised Rose I would go on the ice and help the girls get the hang of skating if they had any issues. Rose had had such a rough few months. She was absolutely smitten with her baby boy, but she was scared. Her mum wasn't the same as before, she knew I was in pain. I had never been one to sit around feeling sorry for myself. Quite the opposite, actually. I was the tough cookie who soldiered on through everything. I had always been a bit of a helicopter parent in the past, but suddenly my little girl, who'd only turned 12 a few short months ago, had needed to grow up so quickly and she'd had to start looking after me. It was meant to be the other way around.

I felt like I'd been letting my sweet girl down for months. For the first time in her life, I was counting on her to do washing and different chores, inside the house and out. Now, before you come at me, she has chores, but the bulk of the general housework sat with me. I was the adult, after all. I also had a particular way that I liked things done, so even if she tried to help me, I preferred to do most of it myself. But I could barely stand for more than a few minutes at a time. I was hunched over when I walked and I no longer recognised myself.

Rose and Mum were basically having to look after me, and they were doing everything for Max except the very basics. It wasn't fair on any of them. I was supposed to look after my girls and my new baby, that was my job and it was a job I took very seriously. It wasn't meant to happen like that.

By the time Sunday morning rolled around, the day of the party, I decided that I was going to skate with Rose and her friends. My niece Ally being one of the kids. I realised that the prolapse had actually happened weeks earlier. Everything from the tenderness in my lower abdomen, to the heaviness and discomfort when I sat down. I wondered if it also explained the pussy discharge that had started a couple of weeks after the operation. I certainly hoped that was nothing more serious.

                        But baby, you're worth it!

I was a nervous wreck from the moment I realised what was happening. I'd barely been able to sleep all weekend but I had gone to bed on the Saturday knowing that we had the party the following day and so I somehow managed to calm myself down enough to get a few hours of shut-eye.

I couldn't cancel Rose's birthday party, she had been through enough over the past few months and so, off we drove, Rose, Ally and myself, at the allocated time. The boot full of party bags and spare clothes each for the girls and me, in case anyone fell and got wet on the ice.

The girls had all arrived in groups, having been car-pooled to the party. I hadn't really spent a lot of time around large groups of kids, certainly not since before Covid. I was feeling quite stressed out about the noise and level of excitement but one of the mums, by the name of Geri, noticed that I was flustered and offered to stay. I barely knew her, other than she was the mum of a lovely quiet girl that Rose had excitedly invited to the party.

Before I knew it, I was confiding in her, telling her what had been happening over the past few months, and in particular about the prolapse that I had just discovered less than 2 days earlier. Geri was horrified. She couldn't believe I had gone ahead with the party but she instantly understood when I had explained that I had to. There was nothing I could do about the prolapse on the weekend and I knew, without needing to be told, that I was probably going to require an operation to fix things. Who knew how long it would take to have things sorted out? I needed Rose to have her special day as planned.

I was so very grateful to Geri, she insisted on staying and helping with the girls. We managed to get through it, 14 girls ice skating and then squealing as they threw their fries at each other afterwards. I was an absolute nervous wreck the whole time but Rose was having too much fun to notice. I was thankful that my little girl was too carefree, too busy enjoying her belated birthday party, to notice my ever-increasing state of anxiety and panic. She would be thrown back into the chaos that had become our world because of my injuries soon enough, but that morning she laughed and squealed just like the other girls.

But baby, you're worth it!

Chapter 12
Monday, 5th September, 2022

After a wonderful weekend it was time to deal with Friday's discovery. The prolapse. I drove Rose to school, she was unusually chirpy for a Monday morning, there was nothing quite like a post party debrief to get a 12-year-old out of bed and she was no exception. It was great to keep my mind off the phone call I needed to make when I got home. The call to re-book my follow-up appointment from the D&C. I had cancelled the appointment for financial reasons. I hadn't been paid from work in a few weeks and had really needed to tighten my belt, so any unnecessary costs had been cut. Never in my wildest dreams did I imagine that there would be any issues after the surgery.

Just after 9am I called the office of the obstetrician who'd done the operation, and briefly explained the situation, asking if there was an emergency opening to see him that week. The only time they could get me in was Wednesday afternoon. The same day as my important interview. I did the math in my head. So long as the interview didn't go for more than an hour, and so long as there was no traffic – I could make it. I needed to make it work, so that's what I'd do.

But first it was time to get to work. I hadn't heard anything official about my colleagues' redundancies, or indeed anything about my own fate. By 1pm I was starting to think maybe I was actually safe. Maybe they had decided to keep me, after all. With that thought in mind I logged in for the weekly regional sales meeting. It was strange, I was the only person on the call from my local team. Management talked about recent changes to the team. I realised that no one had expected me to join the call. They were talking about my role no longer existing. Wow, there was no doubt about it, I wasn't being kept.

Within five minutes of the meeting finishing, I had been sent a calendar request for 9am the following morning. It was from HR and included the VP of the region. There was no mystery there. I'd been made redundant a few times before and the process was always the same. At least I knew it wasn't personal, unlike some of the previous times. The company was closing their Australian office as well as a couple of other regional offices. The sales were not coming in, there was a new CEO and he wasn't wasting any more time, or money, on a dead dog. They were exiting the market. It was no one's fault. It was nothing personal. They'd taken care of me when I'd been so sick. I had nothing but gratitude for that.

Tuesday's meeting went as I knew it would. There was a follow-up call booked for the following Friday and I had the rest of the week off until then. It wasn't ideal, being without a job, but it meant I could have a few more weeks off. That was definitely not a bad thing at that point. I'd broken the golden rule, you see. I had googled it! Yep, I'd googled prolapse symptoms and

But baby, you're worth it!

repair. There was everything from physio to a hysterectomy, and I was sure I'd need the latter.

Any progress I'd made over the past few weeks was starting to crumble. I was normally such a happy and positive person but things were just getting ridiculous. Of course, I had a very important job interview the following day, so at least for the moment I had to somehow figure out how to shelve it and pretend that I wasn't completely terrified. There were bills to pay and there were mouths to feed. Looking after my children was my top priority. But how was I supposed to start a new job in that state, especially if I ended up needing to have an operation? I had always been stubbornly independent, a trait I had inherited from my mum. I had never been one to ask for help, it simply wasn't in my nature.

I was a proud independent woman and my children had rarely wanted for anything, within reason anyway. I didn't know how I was supposed to take care of everyone and provide for them. My thoughts started to spiral but I quickly forced myself back to the present. I had no choice but to smash that interview. I would figure out the rest once I had seen the new doctor and, in the meantime, I would just hope and pray that I was exaggerating, that I was mistaken about what I had discovered, that my internal organs were not really about to fall out of my body.

I spent the afternoon going over my notes from the previous couple of interviews. I had been on both sides of the interview table enough times to know that research was key. Meeting the prospective new boss in person was something I really looked forward to. He was a really easy-going, and down-to-earth guy, and from the first time we'd spoken I knew it would be great to work with him.

Before I knew it, Wednesday arrived. Choosing an outfit took longer than I'd expected. After all, I'd been working from home almost full-time for the past few years. The Covid work from home attire had mostly consisted of a nice top or jumper, depending on the time of year, and either shorts or track pants, or jeans if I was feeling extra fancy.

The exception had been the one day a week that everyone in my previous company, the company I had worked for when I first became pregnant with Max, would come into the office for our Tuesday sales meetings. It had become quite the event. Each week the girls would all be dressed to the nines. I'd be lying if I told you there was a lot of work done, but it had been great fun, I'd really loved the people I worked with at that company. I had to push aside the feeling of sadness that washed over me as I thought about my ex-colleagues. I missed them so much, just as I would miss the people I had been working with for the past few months, but I needed to think positive thoughts with the big interview coming up.

Eventually, I settled on a pink pair of trousers with a black sequin top and black double-breasted jacket with satin lapels. I planned to wear my silver 4-inch stilettos and a few delicate pieces of jewelry. Rose tried to tell me that my outfit was too sparkly and over-the-top, but that was exactly what I was

But baby, you're worth it!

going for. The past few months had taken a massive toll on my confidence and I no longer felt like the confident inked glam Mumma who had worked the room at a conference back in March.

I had been seven months pregnant and on top of the world. There hadn't been many conferences over the previous few years — we all know why. I had been so excited to connect with people face-to-face again. My company had been sponsoring. We had the best swag at the whole event and so people had been lining up to talk to us. It was a fantastic, if not completely exhausting, two days. I'd even talked a guy at another booth into giving me a bright orange motorbike helmet with his company logo on it so I could give it to Rose.

That was the old me. That was the fit and healthy woman, the mum who was on top of the world. I had been so full of life and confidence. I had walked around with my big tummy proudly on display, full of hope for the future. As I stared at my reflection in the mirror, I wondered if that woman would ever find her way back. I conceded that the stranger in the mirror at least looked like me. It was amazing what some skillfully applied makeup, a killer outfit and a hair straightener could do for one's confidence.

An hour later, Rose had been dropped off at school. The interview was not for an hour and a half, so I had plenty of time. The office building that housed the company's Sydney office was about 15 minutes away, I drove to a street around the corner from my destination and pulled over. I was keen to do one more cramming session about the company and the people. Eventually, I decided to stop procrastinating and made my way to a nearby car park.

Almost immediately I regretted my choice of footwear. Whose brilliant idea was it to lay cobblestones in a business district? Some bloke in work boots, no doubt! I made it there in one piece, much to my relief. The interview went well, although I found it difficult to focus on what was being said. There ended up being two other people involved in the interview but they both seemed lovely.

Now that I'd discovered this prolapse, I wondered how on earth it had taken so long to realise what was going on. It was so obvious, I could feel it. When I stood, when I was walking. Holding Max had continued to get more and more uncomfortable. Sitting in that interview, I was sure they could tell there was something wrong with me. I was sure they'd know I was a fake and decide I wouldn't be good enough to do the job.

The interview lasted for just under an hour. I thanked everyone for their time and as soon as I was out of the building I hobbled as fast as I could back to the car. Thankfully, the doctors' rooms were only ten minutes away and I arrived out the front to find half a dozen empty parking spots. Apparently, luck was finally on my side. I added a few coins to the meter and headed towards the building where several specialists had their rooms. I hoped the wait wouldn't be too long. I had to pick Rose up from school in two hours and I had to get home to Max. I missed him so much when I had to leave him.

But baby, you're worth it!

The weather was still pretty cold for early September so I was relieved to find the building was set to the perfect temperature. I lined up at the reception desk to let them know I had arrived before taking a seat in the waiting room. It was about 20 minutes later that the familiar face of the doctor popped around the corner and called my name. I sat down, ready to tell him what had been happening: that I suspected my uterus was literally about to fall out. But he had other things on his mind.

For the next ten minutes, he regaled me with tales of his own children and one in particular's sense of entitlement. Apparently, one of them had done a law degree, all paid for by his parents, who were both medical professionals. The adult child had apparently finished the degree, only to discover that they didn't want to practise law. He was outraged. I couldn't have cared less, I was sitting there, growing more anxious and panicked by the minute.

Finally, I was able to get a few words in, I was able to explain what had happened. To my absolute disbelief, the doctor proceeded to tell me that it was completely normal for your internal organs to collapse from childbirth. I was confused, I couldn't believe what I was hearing.

Finally, it was time to take a look. I hopped on the table as instructed. I was hoping that I was wrong. That I was imagining what I thought I could feel. Unfortunately, it was only a moment before the doctor confirmed the diagnosis. Not only was my uterus about to fall out, but my bladder had also fallen down.

Physiotherapy was mentioned, but somehow, he had misunderstood me when I had explained that I was doing my Kegel exercises, whenever I thought of it. Somehow, he thought I had meant that I couldn't be bothered doing them... Apparently the prolapse was severe enough that it would require surgery regardless of whether I did certain exercises or not.

I was relieved to learn that he was not able to perform the particular surgery I would need himself. As he kept joyfully reminding me that it was completely normal, he gave me a couple of names. I liked the sound of the younger guy who was practising from the same hospital and so he promised to send a referral to the new doctor. He ended up making a phone call and speaking to the doctor as well.

I walked out of that room completely numb. The situation was even worse than I had suspected, and it certainly explained why I was still having issues with incontinence so many months after the birth of my little boy. I didn't understand why that horrible man was so blasé about what had happened. He actually had a big smile on his stupid face as he informed me that it happened to everyone who'd had two babies. Was it really amusing?

He'd joked that I was lucky I'd finished having babies because I wouldn't be able to have any more after the prolapse was fixed. But I wasn't finished. I had my last embryo in storage, waiting. The moment I found out I was pregnant with Max, I had known that I wanted to have my last baby soon after. I was going to give myself 6 months and then I was going to go and have my last embryo transferred, in the hope that I would have another successful pregnancy and my third baby. But now that jerk of a doctor was telling me, gleefully, that my dreams of finally completing the family that I had dreamed of for so long were no longer possible.

It had taken nine years almost to the day, and close to $100k, countless operations and miscarriages to finally get pregnant with Max. I had so many plans for my family which included three children — and in an instant my dreams were shattered. I refused to believe it. That unwelcome piece of news was not part of my plan.

Chapter 13

Monday,
12th September, 2022

When the retained placenta and infection had been discovered and treated, I had, at the advice of a few people close to me, contacted a law firm. The law firm claimed to specialise in birth injury and trauma. The initial conversation had sounded promising. I'd spoken with a young woman and she'd been sympathetic about what I'd been through. I was told that a partner would have a look at my enquiry and someone would contact me, to let me know if I had a case. Eventually, I was told that my mental trauma and pain and suffering were not significant enough to warrant a case. I accepted the news. I was disappointed but I had, or at least I thought I had been, fixed up. I was ready to move on with my life.

Fast forward to a few days after seeing the doctor who had so joyfully told me that my baby-making days were over. I'd been rushed in for an appointment with the doctor who performed the type of surgery I would need. Dr Anderson, he was a Urogynecologist. The moment I sat down in his office I felt at ease. I was so relieved to hear that he didn't find anything funny about what I'd been through. In fact, he was suitably horrified. The new doctor was empathetic and considerate about what I was telling him, such a contrast to the last guy.

Soon enough it was time to hop up on the bed for a little look. Gone was the young woman who would fret for weeks about an upcoming pap smear. I was an old hand at it, the only thing that filled me with dread by that point was the thought of what would be discovered.

Sure enough, it was even worse than I'd been led to believe. There was a prolapse of not only my uterus and bladder, but also my bowel. I shouldn't have been surprised really, I was still losing control of my bowels. I'd never experienced anything like that before, it was absolutely the cherry on top of the shit cupcake that had become my life.

Surgery was the only way to permanently repair the prolapsed organs. My uterus, which was about one centimetre away from falling out of my body, had pulled my bladder and bowel down when it had fallen. I had hoped that the last doctor had been wrong about my ability to have my last baby but unfortunately his advice had been spot-on. Whether or not I had surgery, there was no way my body could handle another pregnancy. I was devastated. How did such a terrible thing happen? I needed answers, I needed to wake up from my horrible nightmare.

There were a couple of options as far as the type of surgery that could be performed. There was the option of repairing the prolapse, meaning my uterus would be sewn back up into place, anchored to some tendon, or something. The other option was a hysterectomy. The latter would be the most straightforward and practical option since I could no longer have another baby. Both surgeries came with a high risk of further issues; there was a lot to weigh up.

The surgery would probably not be done for at least six weeks so Dr Anderson had inserted a pessary, a large rubber-looking ring, which would push everything back up where it was supposed to be until the surgery could be done. I had chosen to have the repair surgery. I understood, at least in theory, that I would never be able to have another baby but I wasn't ready to make such a huge decision. I was not ready to have my womb removed from my body, it just seemed so final. And anyway, I was sure that somehow, once the surgery was performed and I had fully recovered, I would be able to have that last baby after all. Even then, despite everything that I had been through, I still had every intention of having my last baby somehow.

The surgery date could not come quickly enough. We were supposed to fly to Florida for a big family trip to Disney World in mid-September. I had been planning to visit my friend Linda — she had been my boss for a few years and we had remained friends afterwards. My beautiful friend lived not far from Orlando, and she had been so excited about finally meeting my mum and my babies after having seen them on so many early morning conference calls. We had, however, made the disappointing decision to postpone the trip. I was relieved in the end that we had though because it would have been an absolute disaster to go jetting off on a long trip like that.

     But baby, you're worth it!

Max was going through a terrible sleep regression and he was still suffering from the horrible vomiting that had started when he was just a week-and-a-half old. As it turned out, my little boy had severe reflux. Apparently, the reflux had nothing to do with the unnecessary antibiotics that he had been given in the hospital for his eye, a fact that I found hard to believe. He still hated to be in a pram and car seat. There was no way we would have a relaxing trip with everything that had been happening, Plus, there was no way I could complete 30,000 steps a day, as we tended to do on our overseas trips, in the state I was in. I could barely walk to the fridge comfortably.

I'd walked out of the doctor's rooms feeling more positive than I had after seeing that last doctor but I was utterly heartbroken. Dr Anderson had been so gentle and kind about my injuries. But I had been so desperately hoping that he would tell me that the other doctor had been wrong, that I would still be able to have my last baby.

I had kept Rose and Max's newborn clothes. I had spent a fortune renovating our little granny flat over the years. I had room in my home and my heart for three babies, but my dreams had been crushed. I headed home with a heavy heart. The pessary had at least given me instant relief physically. I could walk properly again, the heaviness was almost completely gone, as was the distension in my lower belly. But it wasn't to last.

The next morning, I hopped out of bed, full of hope but I immediately knew that the pessary had failed. I went to the bathroom and pushed it back up as I'd been directed to do, should it slip down. But I could not for the life of me get it back to the position that it had been placed in by the doctor. The relief had been short-lived. As were my plans to go for a walk down by the harbour with mum that day. I was instantly annoyed with myself for even entertaining the thought. I swore to myself that, once I was all better, I would never take simple things like a leisurely walk for granted again.

One thing I was still relieved about, however, was the doctor's reassurance that my prolapse was not normal. He completely agreed that it had been caused by a combination of the untreated infection and the incorrect use of forceps. With that news, I believed that there was a renewed case of negligence, so once the clock struck nine that following morning, a few hours after I realised that the pessary had failed, I decided to call the law firm once more.

Things had definitely become more serious. I spoke with the same young woman that I had spoken to a couple of months before, and she believed there may be a way for me to get some kind of compensation after all. My baby was over four months of age, I had never been able to hold him without some kind of pain or discomfort — pain and discomfort that had actually been caused by those forceps, and indeed the retained placenta and infection. It was nothing to do with my age, it could have happened to anyone. A 25-year-old woman's body would not have been able to with take what I'd been through, any more than my body had been able to.

                    But baby, you're worth it!

It was only a couple of days before I heard back from the principal of the medical legal team. We spoke for almost an hour, and by the end of the call she was in agreement. We would need to wait until I had had the operation before they could make a definite call either way. But she agreed that there was likely a breach by the hospital in their duty of care. I was asked to provide any medical records and medical bills, of which there were many at that point. Once my operation had been performed, hopefully in the next few weeks, we should be able to take things further. I ended the call and realised that I was smiling from ear to ear for what seemed like the first time in months.

I felt like that woman had my back, that she was going to fight for some kind of justice. Nothing would take away the terrible pain or mental anguish I'd endured. Nothing would give me back those precious few months with my children, in particular the months that I couldn't even cuddle my new baby comfortably. I hadn't been able to fully immerse myself in my little boy, like I had when Rose had been a baby. I felt like I'd been ripped off, I'd missed out on all that wonderful enjoyment this time around.

But finally, I felt like maybe, just maybe, things would be okay.

Chapter 14
Friday, 21ˢᵗ October, 2022

Life went on after my appointment with Doctor Anderson. As promised, the prolapse remained the same. I had been terrified that things would get worse but as promised, they didn't. I knew that I had several weeks to wait until the surgery was due to go ahead. The date hadn't been locked in, but it looked like mid-October was the likely time frame.

Rose was the most easygoing child that I had ever encountered, she had been since she was just a baby. She would happily eat and sleep anywhere and everywhere. Max, on the other hand, had been a much more full-on baby. My little sweet boy still hated the pram and the car seat just as he had from day one. He hated being put down at all, in fact. By the time my prolapse had been discovered and then diagnosed I was starting to wonder what I was doing wrong. I had been in such a bad way since his birth but I loved and adored him so very much.

Nothing I did seemed to make him happy, though. Of course, the terrible reflux wasn't helping the situation. We had been to a local shopping centre a couple of weeks before the prolapse was discovered, intent on doing some clothes

                    But baby, you're worth it!

shopping for Rose and Brittany. But Max had screamed the place down within minutes of arriving and so I had ended up sending Mum, Rose and Brittany off to do their shopping while I made my way with Max to the parents' room to change and feed him.

Once I had put two change mats down, to protect my baby from any germs, I carefully laid Max down but quickly realised that I had brought the wrong size nappies. I hadn't taken my baby out of the house for so long that I hadn't realised that the nappies in his bag were a couple of sizes too small. Thankfully a lovely young couple who I'd been chatting with while we waited for the change tables to become free, offered me one of their daughter's nappies. The little girl was a few months older than Max but thankfully they wore the same size nappies. This small but much-needed act of kindness was the end of me.

Tears began silently rolling down my cheeks. I wiped them away, embarrassed that I'd let anyone see me in such a moment of weakness. But once they'd gathered up their belongings and strapped their little girl back into her pram, and headed for the door, I began to sob. I had really been looking forward to taking my little guy shopping. It was one of my favourite pastimes, wandering aimlessly around that shopping centre, collecting a few random things that I didn't need, eating in the food court that overlooked the ice rink. Instead of wandering around the shops we sat in that parents' room, changing then feeding my precious boy and I cried. I cried and cried.

People came in and out, no one even seemed to even notice the woman sitting, quietly sobbing as she fed her little baby. I felt invisible. I realised at that moment that I'd become disconnected from the rest of the world. I had wanted my sweet little baby for so long, and I loved him so very much, but at the same time I had started to resent him. I was sure he hated me, why else would he cry so much? I felt like he knew that I was broken and not good enough to be his mother. It was utterly heartbreaking.

Max still had to be held upright for at least half an hour after his bottles, and even then, he would often vomit, and so I was also constantly stressed that my little boy must surely be losing too much weight. Thankfully, whenever we had an appointment with the baby health nurse, his weight and height were tracking perfectly along the 85th percentile. He was tracking along the same line that he had been at birth and even before that, during my pregnancy.

Everything just seemed so much harder than it was supposed to be, but I tried to push my doubts aside because my precious little baby and my big girl were my world. I reminded myself, whenever those doubts started to push their way into my subconscious, that everything would be okay once my operation was done. I would be okay, and I was sure that Max would sense that things were finally normal. I was sure that my little boy would start to love me the way that I loved him. It had occurred to me many times over those months that for the first time ever, I needed a guy to love me, even if he just had a fraction of the love that I had for him.

  But baby, you're worth it!

I had tried not to think too much about the tiny embryo that I had still in storage. The little frostie, as I referred to it. When I was first planning my embryo transfer, after finding out about the NK cells, I had been so excited. I had always imagined having twins. One of my miscarriages had actually been twins. I had started bleeding about 7 weeks into the pregnancy, at first it was no more than light spotting and so I had hoped and prayed that everything would be okay but the bleeding soon became heavier. The bleeding had happened on a Saturday, I still remember it like it was yesterday.

I had spent the weekend in agony. That familiar period-like cramping that comes with a miscarriage as your cervix contracts, trying to rid the body of the failed pregnancy. It hurt, but nowhere near as much as my heart did. It was the first time I had managed to actually become pregnant after Rose was born. About 4 years after I had started trying for my second baby. I had taken it for granted that those 2 lines on the pregnancy test would automatically mean I would meet my baby some 8 months later.

I had gone for blood tests the following week which confirmed that my pregnancy had been lost but then to my absolute joy and excitement the hormone levels mysteriously started rising again. The joy and excitement were fleeting though when a couple of weeks later, I started bleeding again. It turned out that I had been pregnant with twins but had then gone on to lose the second baby as well.

That miscarriage took about 7 weeks from start to finish. It was the most horrible, soul crushing experience, and one that

I vowed to never let myself go through again. For a while I was ready to give up on my dream of giving Rose a sibling because I didn't want to risk having to go through that again. I had been so sure that I was going to have twins when I first started trying for my second baby and so to have had, and then lost, those twins, was absolutely soul crushing.

When I had been preparing for my embryo transfer with Max, I initially wanted to use both of my remaining embryos at the same time, to finally have my twins. The fertility specialist had talked me out of it, though. There was an increased risk with a twin pregnancy, especially at my age. There was also the possibility that if one of the babies miscarried, there was a high risk that the other one would as well. That last fact was enough to convince me that having a singleton was a perfectly wonderful idea.

And so, I made a plan, that if I was successful first go, I would have that baby and then transfer the last embryo when, as it turned out, he, was about 6 months old. I had been so distraught upon finding out that I could no longer have another baby. I was ever conscious of my little frostie, but I had no choice but to try and push those thoughts to the back of my mind.

I had so much on my plate that I had managed not to think about that last baby until about a week after my appointment with Doctor Anderson. I was scrolling through my emails, as I did a few dozen times a day when, all of a sudden, I noticed an address that stopped me in my tracks. It was the email address of my fertility clinic. I tapped the email to open it because they

   But baby, you're worth it!

sometimes sent me newsletters and random information and so I figured it would be another one of those emails. But it wasn't. My heart dropped to my toes as I read the text. It was a direct debit notification for my embryo storage fees.

I had been receiving those notifications every 6 months for a long time. I had set up the direct debit to make sure that I didn't miss an invoice or forget to pay. That future little baby was far too important to risk losing because of an invoice that had ended up in my spam folder or something. The last notification had come in the weeks before Max was born, when I was happily oblivious to what was soon to unfold in that delivery theatre.

I was sitting on my lounge holding my sweet baby while he slept, and on reading that email I finally had to face the fact. There was a very real possibility that I may have to let my dream of another baby go. That I might have to let go of my embryo, but how? I had fought so hard to have my little Max. I had gone through so much to have those two tiny embryos frozen, years earlier. I had been so very lucky to have success the first time we had tried the immune protocol. A lot of women have to try a few different protocols, changing the type and amount of the drugs that were administered, to find the winning formula. But I had been lucky, my highly skilled specialist had insisted on a much gentler regime than what I had gone to her with, having googled myself into a frenzy. And it had paid off.

How on earth was I going to just accept defeat? I had fought so hard, and I was still fighting every day, fighting to get my health back and rallying to make sure my kids were loved and looked

after, despite what I was going through. I am far from perfect;
I have a lot of faults just like anyone else does.

One thing I most certainly am not though, is a quitter. I will
see things through to the end, whether it was a task that
I thoroughly enjoyed or something that scared me or just filled
me with dread, I would see it through. I had not come all that
way to quit. I may not have met that baby yet but I was going to
fight for them, just like I would do for Rose and Max every day,
and twice on a Sunday, as the saying goes.

The thought terrified me, but that evening, once Max was
happily sleeping beside me, I unlocked my phone and began
the daunting task of researching surrogacy in Australia. I had
an idea of how things worked already. I had actually had a
plan, all those years ago, when I had headed along to that
first fertility clinic. I was going to have my second and third
babies quickly, if not at the same time. Once my family was
complete, I was going to donate my eggs to a couple of women
who were unable to use their own eggs for whatever reason,
and then, I was going to consider becoming a surrogate,
probably for a gay man or gay couple, since women were
already more than capable of carrying their own children, or
so I had thought until recently. I researched how I would go
about doing both of those things in the early days, all those
years ago. But as time went on and my struggle to conceive
became all encompassing, my desire to help other people
waned. I had realised that if I couldn't have my own babies
then I wasn't exactly going to be a suitable candidate to help
other people.

                                    But baby, you're worth it!

I was disappointed and more than a bit surprised to see that nothing much had changed in the ten years since I had first looked into surrogacy. I knew that commercial surrogacy, where the intended parent, or parents, entered into a business arrangement with the surrogate, was still illegal in Australia. The only option available in our country was altruistic surrogacy. Meaning that there was to be no payment to a surrogate for carrying the baby. Medical bills and other reasonable expenses, such as time off work and travelling to and from appointments, would be reimbursed but that was it.

As an intended parent you could not buy gifts or anything else that could be construed as a form of payment. The surrogate, despite giving up their body to grow a human infant, only to give that infant up once they were born, was not allowed to receive so much as an extravagant bunch of flowers without a good reason, in case it was seen as a form of payment.

I stumbled across a case where a surrogate had felt so connected to the baby they were carrying that they decided, upon the birth of the child, they could not bear to give the baby to the biological parents. The case had no clear outcome that I could find but I was confused. To my absolute horror, I read on to discover that when the child was born, the surrogate woman, and her partner if she had one, were considered to be the legal parents of the child. The child would be handed over to the intended parents as a matter of course, if the surrogate agreed to it but the biological or "intended" parents had to go through the process of adopting their child. This was the case regardless of whether the surrogate had used her own eggs, or indeed an embryo that had been created with the intended parent's DNA.

I could see why there were so many articles about finding a close friend or relative to carry a baby for you. The risk of having your surrogate decide that they wanted to keep the baby would be massively reduced when the baby was carried by someone who would be able to have an ongoing family, or at least close connection, with the child and parent, or parents.

I decided to search to see what the rules were elsewhere in the world. Sure enough, commercial surrogacy was allowed in places like the US and parts of Europe. Having spent a lot of time in the US over the years I knew that if I were to go down that route, it would definitely make the most sense to use an American surrogate. I had so many close friends in places like Austin, Detroit, California and, of course, Florida — and so any excuse to see them would be a huge bonus as well.

California seemed to be the place to go but that also meant a huge expense. I would have to have my embryo sent to one of the clinics there, and there were dozens. The surrogate would be a young woman. The more experienced surrogates attracted a premium fee. All up, the cost would be well over $100k, and from what I could see, that was in US currency, not Australian.

It was a depressing thought, the time and money that would be involved. If I decided to try and find a surrogate in Australia

But baby, you're worth it!

then I was limited. Most of my close friends were my age, after all. I had a few cousins and other close family members that I could ask, but how on earth would I ever work up the courage to do so? The other option would be to have a stranger carry my baby in another country, halfway around the world.

I wouldn't be able to check in on them, help them through the hard parts of their pregnancy like morning sickness in the early weeks, and then those final weeks when you can barely put your shoes on, let alone clean the house. I had always loved any excuse to jump on a plane to the US, I had been there 11 times and had so many more trips planned in the future, but it wasn't exactly a quick trip across the pacific. And, of course, Max was so little, it occurred to me that there was no way he would cope with a 15-hour flight.

I had to bring myself back to the present then. I reminded myself that even if I was able to go ahead with finding a surrogate, it would be at least a few months before I could even start the process. I had to figure out how on earth I could pay for it for a start. I had the income from the investment but it was a small beach bungalow up the coast, not a mansion in Mosman worth millions. My financial plan had included money for one more round of IVF and the immune medications to go with my last embryo transfer. Suddenly the $5k treatment that I'd planned for was going to cost up to twenty times that. I had planned to start saving again as soon as I was back at work when Max was a few weeks old, but instead I had needed the income to supplement my wage and pay for the extensive medical bills that I had incurred because of my injuries. My mum had offered to give me her share to pay for everything, but she was retired and I knew that she relied on that money. Plus, I was far too proud to accept it.

Luckily, I knew that I could probably still stretch my savings and the wage from my new job to afford either of the options. I had the money from my last redundancy which was supposed to pay for the Florida trip that we'd had to cancel as well. Thinking about the money side of things was a bit depressing, so I decided that I'd seen enough for the time being.

I knew that I had a lot to think about. I wanted to talk to people who had used a surrogate, both in Australia and in the US, but it was late. I knew that most people with young children would be sensible enough to be asleep that late at night, unlike me, so there was unlikely to be anyone online to answer my questions anyway.

Of course, my brain was running at a million miles an hour and so I jumped onto messenger to check in with my friend Dani. She was one of my close friends who lived in the UK and she was heading back to Sydney for the first time in nearly 15 years. Dani was due to arrive in late October and was bringing her husband, Andy, and their son, Will. I was keen to update her on our preparations for their visit. I had already let her know that my surgery would likely happen about a week before they arrived but I had assured her that I would be back up and about well before they touched down in Sydney.

　　　　　　　　　But baby, you're worth it!

My friend's impending visit was a light at the end of that cold dark tunnel I'd been stuck in for months. In a matter of weeks, I would be all better and living my best life with one of my dearest friends. I couldn't wait.

Chapter 15
Saturday, 22nd October, 2022

Mid-October came and went. I was so disappointed that I still hadn't had my surgery. I didn't even have a date locked in the calendar yet. When I first met with Dr Anderson, he had suggested that my surgery would be sometime in mid-October and I had asked to be placed on the cancellation wait list, hoping that the surgery would be done even sooner. I had stuck with my original plan, to have the repair surgery rather than the hysterectomy. The surgery would likely need to be re-done after about 10 years anyway, and so I had decided that I would have the more major surgery next time. My children would no longer be small and wanting to curl up on my lap by then and so it seemed like the perfect plan.

I was finally given a date. That late October list had fallen through, and so the soonest I could have the surgery would be Tuesday 15th November. Just a week and a half after my friends had returned home from their visit. It wasn't ideal that I would have to wait another month, although in a way I was almost starting to learn to live with the prolapse, which hadn't got any worse.

Apparently, plenty of women lived with the same injuries. I couldn't imagine that though. How did women exercise or run after their children? And how on earth did anybody have sex in that state? It wasn't a problem I had to deal with at the time. I was a single woman after all, with a 12-year-old and a baby who was only a few months old. But what about women who were married or partnered? At least when I was ever ready to date again this would be all fixed up. I was sure that one day my Prince Charming would finally show up after all.

I tried to focus on the positives. Although I wouldn't be able to lift Max for a few weeks, I would only be in hospital and away from my babies for one night. I had decided that I was going to try and get home that night, just as I had all those months earlier after the D&C to remove the retained placenta. I had always considered myself to be pretty tough and the surgery didn't sound too complicated. I figured I would be up and about within a few hours of the surgery. The doctors would be so impressed by how well I was doing that they would send me home to get on with my life. The surgery was going to be performed mostly laparoscopically, after all.

So, although I was disappointed that I wouldn't be all fixed up for Dani and the boy's arrival, I tried to focus on their visit. We had planned all sorts of exciting outings in the couple of weeks that they would be in Sydney. Our friends were going to be arriving late on the Friday and the plan was for them to come over for an early dinner the following night, after they had spent the morning and early afternoon sightseeing, since Andy and Will had never been to Australia before.

Rose and my nieces, Ally and Brittany, spent the Friday and most of Saturday cleaning up the yard, sweeping and just generally helping to tidy the houses, both mine and mum's, ready for our guests. Mum was fantastic as always, cooking up a storm for our visitors. I felt terrible about not being able to help but between my injuries and Max's refusal to be put down for more than a couple of minutes at a time, with the exception of his naps, I really wasn't much help to anyone.

Mum and Rose had been looking after Max and I for such a long time that I started to feel utterly useless. I had managed to at least shop for the food and drinks when I had taken Rose to school a couple of days earlier, and so felt like I had done something to contribute.

When my friends knocked on our gate at 2pm that day it instantly felt like no time had passed. Max was asleep inside with Mum and so for the first hour of their visit we talked and laughed, sharing some of the wonderful memories we had from the trip that Rose and I had taken to visit them in the UK some four-and-a-half years earlier. Our plan had been to see each other every two years but that was just one more thing that Covid had messed up.

We made all sorts of wonderful plans for the two weeks they were going to be here with us. The first outing would be a drive out to the Blue Mountains the following Monday, Dani had never been out there to see those majestic mountains, blanketed in gum trees. The eucalyptus oil gives the trees a blue appearance from a distance, hence the name. Of course,

   But baby, you're worth it!

Mum's car was big enough to take her and Max with us as well, but I preferred not to take my baby so far from home. I was becoming more and more anxious about taking Max out, even though he was starting to come around to the pram and the car seat. I was terrified of my baby getting sick or hurt out in the big bad world; he was far safer at home.

About an hour after Dani and the boys arrived, Max woke up. And he was instantly in love with his new friends with the funny accents. Andy rolled his eyes and laughed as he teased Dani for being so clucky. I was so thrilled that they'd had a chance to meet Max as a baby, unlike the bigger kids, who had been about 8 when we'd last caught up. We'd shared many pictures and sent gifts, but nothing beat actual baby cuddles.

Mum and the girls went to fetch the food while my friends became better acquainted with the sweet baby they'd heard so much about. Dinner was as wonderful as the company. Mum had outdone herself as always. I had bought sushi and doughnuts for the kids, knowing that Will was as fussy an eater as Rose was. Even Max, who had started on solids just a few weeks earlier, was getting right into the party spirit. He even sat happily in his highchair for the first time ever. I had never seen my little fellow so happy.

Lunch went far too quickly and before we knew it, it had gone 6pm. Max was ready for his bedtime bottle and Dani and the boys were having trouble keeping their eyes open. Plus, Mum had been working nonstop between looking after me and getting the food and garden ready. I didn't want my friends to have to catch a ride share so I sorted little Max out with his bottle, which Mum would give him while I ran our guests back to their hotel. I'd be back in half an hour or so. Which meant that Mum could still have a relatively early night, and hopefully a sleep-in the following morning.

We piled into the car, Rose, myself and our visitors. Everyone was sad for the evening to end, but we knew we had plenty of time over the next two weeks to catch up. We talked excitedly on the way to their hotel about the snacks I had bought for our car trip to the Blue Mountains. I realised as I drove home afterwards that I had actually gone several hours without thinking about everything that was coming up: Max's constant crying, my operation, and the reality that I was going to have to try to find a surrogate if I was going to try for my last, longed-for baby.

I hopped into bed that night, feeling truly content for the first time in months. Max was exhausted and fell asleep quickly. As I slept that night I had the most wonderful dream. We were in Paris. I was laughing at my mum, she was buying ice-cream for herself and the kids. She was attempting to speak French with an old man who had an ice-cream cart on the Champ de Mars. I was intrigued though because I recognised Max with his fiery red hair and those stunning blue eyes that crinkled when he smiled. Then, of course, there was Rose and my niece Ally.

The girls looked the same, if not far too grown up. But then there was a tiny boy of about two. The little boy had the same blue eyes as the rest of us, and the distinctive red hair that my

　　　　　　　　　　But baby, you're worth it!

children had inherited from my mum. I was trying to figure out where he had come from. When suddenly Brittany's voice broke through my thoughts. She was calling my name, but it didn't make any sense. Brittany wasn't there. I tried to see the little boy again but the sound of my niece, banging and knocking on my door woke me from my lovely dream and into a nightmare.

Chapter 16
Sunday, 23rd October, 2022

My mum was sick; she needed an injection. Max was still asleep, but Rose had also been woken by Brittany's frantic screaming. I jumped out of bed, leaving Rose with instructions to talk to the baby if he woke up before I got back.

My mum has something called Meniere's Disease, you see. It's hard to explain the disease as I don't fully understand it myself, but I can tell you that when my mum has an attack, she can vomit for anywhere between one and forty-eight hours and she cannot walk for the severe dizziness. Watching my normally active and vibrant mother unable to pick herself up off the bathroom floor for hours, moaning as the waves of nausea battered her like waves constantly pounding on cliffs, and knowing there was nothing I could do for her was unbearable.

I still remember her very first attack, about five years earlier. I was at work when I received a panicked call from our neighbour. He was calling to let me know that my mum was violently ill and needed me to get home as soon as possible.

By the time I returned home, Mum had been taken in an ambulance to the hospital. She had been so sick that she was terrified she might die. My brothers and I had raced up with the kids to see her but the hospital couldn't figure out what was wrong. Several hours and two nausea injections later, she was sent home.

Everything was fine for a couple of weeks but then the attacks started to happen more and more often. At first, the doctors concluded that she was suffering from vertigo, but eventually, after suffering with fairly regular attacks for about 18 months, she was diagnosed with Meniere's Disease.

The specialist who diagnosed Mum's Meniere's Disease was able to prescribe an injection that could be administered when the symptoms began. At first, Mum didn't know how she was ever going to get someone to come and give her an injection. Until I reminded my mum that I had given myself hundreds of injections over the years whilst trying to conceive Max. I was more than capable of giving her a needle if I needed to.

Eventually the symptoms all but stopped, becoming nothing more than an occasional bout of light headedness. Everyone closest to her was relieved that Mum seemed to have been cured. Or so we thought. That attack after my friends visit in late October was the worst one she had ever had. It lasted for almost 48 hours and even the needles did nothing to make her feel better until the attack had finally run its course.

Over the next couple of weeks, mum had attacks every two or three days. It was absolutely devastating watching my mum go through those attacks, knowing there was nothing I could do to make her feel better. The medications still weren't working for some reason. Mum tried to put it down to the fact that she'd grown complacent with tracking her salt consumption, but I knew that her main trigger had always been stress, and this time was no different. The last few months had taken more of a toll on her than I could ever have imagined. It was my fault that her attacks had started again.

We had to cancel our day in the Blue Mountains, I couldn't risk being two hours away, even if I had taken Max with us, and there was no way I was doing that. I couldn't cope with him getting upset when I didn't have Mum there to help me. It made me panic at the best of times. I needed to somehow look after everyone. I needed to be at home. I ended up keeping Rose home from school for a few days, which wasn't ideal, but I didn't know how to juggle looking after Mum, Max and doing the school runs. Poor Rose had already had to grow up so much since my issues had started. I can't imagine how hard it was for her, but she stepped up far beyond anything I could have hoped for.

Thankfully, Mum had days where she was perfectly fine. I had to play it by ear as far as any plans we made with Dani and the boys, which they completely understood. We managed to go to the zoo the first week they were here, then after they returned from seeing friends up the coast, we had a great time taking the kids trick or treating for Halloween. Even Max dressed up in a

But baby, you're worth it!

little black onesie with bats on it and was a huge hit with all of the neighborhood kids.

My birthday was a couple of days before my impending surgery but we had decided to celebrate it the weekend before Dani and the boys returned to the UK. That weekend arrived far too quickly. I was excited about having dinner with my immediate family and my dear friends but I was dreading having to say goodbye.

Still, I had booked the function room at Attimo, a wonderful Italian restaurant I'd discovered the previous year while planning a big milestone birthday for my mum. I had become a regular customer and became friends with the owner, David, and his staff. Dani was excited to have a meal there since she hadn't been able to attend my baby shower, which had also been held there in March, just a couple of months before Max had arrived.

Dinner was a success. The food was delicious, and the conversation was light and fun. Max was almost six months old and so he was allowed to try a few mouthfuls of mashed up lasagna, which was a massive hit. It was such an exhausting affair that my tired boy even slept in his carrier for an hour, meaning that we could stay a little later than what we'd originally anticipated.

The following day we had been planning to meet one of my Mum's cousins for lunch at a nearby cafe but we had cancelled it just in case mum was unwell. I was convinced that the dinner the evening before would cause Mum to have an attack. I had even tried to cancel the dinner several times but Mum would not hear of it. She had, however, agreed to postpone the lunch, just in case it was too much.

Dani was planning to get a small tattoo that morning as a momento of her trip. Her plan was to wait until the last day so it wouldn't interfere with her swimming and enjoying the sunshine while she was here. Mum had been feeling good for a couple of days and so, once Max was ready for his morning sleep, she insisted that Rose and I should go and see our friends once more before they left to go back home.

I felt guilty at first, insisting that I was happy to spend the day looking after Mum and the kids, and doing some cleaning but, once again, Mum insisted I go and spend time with my friends while I had the chance. Eventually, I agreed to go out for 2 hours, promising to be back before Max was due for his next bottle. With that, I kissed my tiny boy and headed for the door with Rose excitedly hurrying along in front of me.

I toyed with the idea of getting a tattoo myself. It had been a few years since I'd had any ink; it was yet another thing that Covid had interfered with. It occurred to me that it would probably be another few years before we would get the chance to do it again and so, with Rose's help, I chose a design that symbolised our friendship perfectly.

The tattoos were finished a lot quicker than I expected. We were in and out in less than half an hour. I had assumed that

          But baby, you're worth it!

I would have enough time to accompany Dani to get her tattoo done before grabbing a quick takeaway and heading home. With another hour and a half before I had to head home, we decided to grab lunch at a nearby pub.

Lunch was over far too quickly. The pub was almost empty and so the kids happily sat themselves at a separate table. It was lovely to see Rose enjoying her friend's company. There was only three months' difference in their age and so they had a lot in common despite living on different ends of the planet. It struck me again how much Rose had grown up over the previous six months, but I pushed the thoughts aside, deciding to just enjoy watching her have fun. Before we knew it, we had finished our meal and were pulling up outside the hotel.

The days I spent with Dani and the boys were the only time I'd felt normal in months. There was no screaming baby, no sick Mum, just me and my Rose. But in a few short minutes they'd be gone, and I would be plunged back into what had become my miserable reality. I couldn't see the happy future that I'd envisioned during my pregnancy, or in those first couple of weeks after Max was born.

Dani and I hugged and promised each other that we wouldn't leave it for four years again. We promised each other that we wouldn't cry, and I kept that last promise for about two minutes. As Rose and I drove away, I began to cry, and I cried all the way home. I cried all afternoon, and for the next couple of days.

Chapter 17

Wednesday,
9th November, 2022

I hadn't got around to cancelling my operation yet but I couldn't possibly go ahead with it while Mum was so sick. On the Wednesday after my friends had returned home, Max was booked in for his six-months check-up with the local baby health clinic. I'd taken Rose for many check-ups there when she'd been a baby and toddler so I knew that these wonderful women were trustworthy. Max was checked over, weighed and measured and, as I already knew, he was perfect.

Unfortunately, or in hindsight, fortunately, the nurse wanted to know how I was going. I blurted it all out and once again I began to sob. I assured her that I loved my little boy more than life itself, and I did, with all my heart. But I wasn't okay. I realised at that moment that I hadn't been okay for months.

Mum's illness was literally the straw that had broken the camel's back. I had hit rock bottom. I'd basically alienated myself from everyone outside the bubble that was my household. I was so ashamed of what had been happening, of how I had been feeling that I couldn't possibly tell anyone.

I was the happy one who wore cowboy boots and far too many sequins. I was the one who took care of people when they needed to smile. I had tried for so long to have my perfect little baby, and there was no way I could admit that my life with him was anything other than the perfect fairytale everyone thought it was. I couldn't be the weak one who needed help. I wouldn't have known how to be vulnerable if I tried, it was something I had never allowed myself to be.

Thankfully, that lady saw straight through me. She told me that it was okay to feel so overwhelmed. Anyone who'd been through what I had over the past six months would be a nervous wreck. Here I was with my beautiful and perfect little chubby baby, he was clearly so loved. I should give myself a break, she told me. There was certainly nothing to be ashamed of.

I told the lovely nurse that I would be taking Max to the GP the following day for his six-month injections. She asked if she could call and speak to the doctor. I guess she wanted to explain that I wasn't doing too well, in case I didn't tell them myself. She needn't have worried, this woman's empathy as well as the absolute shock that I was still a functioning human being, at least to look at, made me realise that, if not for myself, then at least for Mum and my babies, I needed to get some help.

That evening, I posted anonymously on a local mums' group that I was a part of. I asked if anyone had advice about where I could get some help looking after Mum and maybe around the house. I posted anonymously because I didn't want any of my friends, all of whom were in this group, to know that it was me.

Within a couple of hours two of my best friends, Lindsay and Chelsea, had messaged me.

The girls had seen the post and immediately knew it had been written by me. My beautiful friends had been worried about me for months, but they had their own families and challenges. These women had been like sisters to me for over 25 years and so they had assumed I would ask them for help if I needed it. On top of the message from my friends, I had an overwhelming response to the post. Many people suggested a nanny or daycare but there was no way I was trusting someone I didn't know with my precious boy, that simply was not an option.

Among the women who had responded were a few people who had mums or partners with Meniere's Disease. All of whom mentioned a drug I'd never heard of, and I was fairly certain that Mum hadn't heard of it either, or at least that she wasn't taking it. So, I immediately researched it. I told Mum about the medication that evening, and we agreed that I would get her a script for it the next morning when Max went for his needles. We were feeling hopeful, maybe Mum could get over the horrible attacks once and for all.

The following morning, Max and I drove Rose to school before heading over to the doctor. I'd received an email the evening before but hadn't actually seen it until that morning. I finally got around to reading the email just before we left the house. Rose had been accepted into the talented and gifted program at the high school she was starting at the following year. To say that I was proud would be a gross understatement.

 But baby, you're worth it!

My sweet girl had experienced a rough time at school. She'd had some nasty teachers, and others who just couldn't be bothered. She'd copped a hard time from some nasty kids as well, and then there'd been the absolute shit storm that had been home learning during Covid. I had been working 12-hour days at the time and so Mum had helped Rose as much as possible, but she'd fallen behind like so many other kids. It had been clear from very early on that she was a very bright child, so it confused me that she was having trouble learning.

Everything changed when we moved her to a small school about 20 minutes away from home at the start of year five. The class was much smaller than what we were used to, with only 25 kids. Rose instantly befriended a group of lovely girls, and the parents were also lovely, none of the stuck-up crap we'd experienced at her first school. But the thing that stood out to me almost immediately was the teacher, Eliza James.

Mrs. James was absolutely brilliant, she was empathetic, kind, compassionate but, most importantly, she saw Rose for the highly intelligent child that I'd always known she was. We were over the moon to learn that Rose would have her again for year six. That beautiful lady had played a huge part in her achievement and Rose absolutely could not wait to tell her all about it, so off she went with a spring in her step and the biggest smile on her sweet face.

Twenty minutes later, I had parked the car and loaded Max and the 57 items needed for a quick outing, into the pram. We waited a little over an hour and were finally ushered into the doctor's room. Little Max was so very brave, a little cry and then he was all better. Of course, Max's cries had set me off, and I told the doctor that things had been going from bad to worse at home. As it turned out, she had spoken with the nurse the day before and she wanted me to start taking antidepressants straight away.

This doctor had known me a long time and she knew that I was usually pretty resilient. I don't know if she'd actually ever seen me cry before. I knew I needed to get a handle on things now before they got any worse, and so I agreed. I walked out with my script as well as one for the new medication for Mum. Thankfully, the doctor had totally agreed and as it turned out that particular drug was actually developed to help control the symptoms associated with Ménière's Disease.

A quick trip to the chemist and Max and I were headed home. I was ready to get myself and my mum better. Mum was waiting in the driveway as I drove in a few short minutes later. She was keen to know what the doctor had said, and to see her boy after his yukky needles. I could see the relief on her face as I handed her the box of pills, and she took one immediately, as I did with mine.

So much had happened over the last couple of weeks since Mum had her first attack, well the first one in such a long time, at least. It had been such a hectic time between the attacks, having our friends here from the UK and trying to take care of my mum and children. I still hadn't got around to postponing my operation. I had learned to live with the heaviness in my

          But baby, you're worth it!

belly and the horrible feeling in my groin so for now I was sure that I could ignore it. But I was starting my new job in about nine weeks. I forgot to tell you that I was offered, and of course accepted, my dream job.

The GP had strongly suggested going ahead with the operation, while I had the time off to fully recover. Mum wasn't taking no for an answer. Her new medication had taken effect immediately. I would not be allowed to lift baby for the first six weeks, I already knew that. Because the surgery was being done laparoscopically, I figured I knew what I was in for. We would have my younger brother Nick staying in the flat downstairs while I was in hospital for the night, just in case Mum needed an injection. The fridge and freezer were full for a week or so, in case I couldn't drive for a few days. So, the following Monday morning, the day before the operation, I finally agreed that going ahead would be the right thing to do.

Chapter 18

Tuesday, 15th November, 2022

I finally received my fasting instructions late the night before the operation. I could eat until 9am the next morning, and a sip of water here and there as needed until 1pm. I was due to be at the hospital at 2pm. Rose was getting a couple of days off school. It was too much for Mum to have to run around with the kids and to risk an attack, so the plan was for Rose to spend a big chunk of those two days working on her last school project for the year. Everyone was awake by 6:30am as usual. Breakfast was quite the affair with all sorts of unnecessary treats for me. I'm not sure what it is but something about not being allowed to eat for a few hours always caused me to panic eat, add a few extra layers of fat.

By 1:45pm I had checked a hundred times that Mum was okay, I'd kissed my babies about 700 times, I was still feeling like I was doing the wrong thing. Mum had finally started feeling better again for the first time in almost a month, but it was too late to back out. It would be okay, though, I'd be back home the following day and Nick was perfectly capable of handling anything that came up that night or in the morning. I expected

But baby, you're worth it!

to be home by the following lunchtime. I'd made up bags with vials of mum's injections along with syringes and needles, gloves and pieces of disposable baby change mats that I'd cut into squares, to lay everything out on. I had gone into great detail with Nick a few days earlier about how to break the vials and tap the air out of the syringes. My brother was more than a bit nervous about the prospect of having to give Mum an injection but I knew that if anyone could get it done, it was him.

We finally drove away in Nick and his wife Skye's little green frog car. It was a strange experience being in such a tiny car after driving an SUV for so many years. We chatted easily. I couldn't tell you what we talked about, but knowing us it was probably about upcoming holidays. If there was one thing we had in common, other than our obsession with the Rabbitohs, it was our love of travel. We had spent a few days sightseeing in Paris a few years earlier, during the same trip that Rose and I had spent a few days with Dani and the boys up in the UK. Our time in Paris had been absolutely magical and we were hoping to take Mum, my kids, the nieces and his son Jonathan in the next couple of years.

Nick pulled up at the hospital all too soon. He knew I was having serious second thoughts but assured me he would take care of Mum and the kids. I knew he would, and so with that I hopped out of the car with my tiny suitcase, the same one I'd re-packed a few days before I had gone to be induced with my little Max, a million years ago.

The same hospital where I'd had the retained placenta and subsequent infection treated. It was hard to believe it had been four months since then. I had walked out of here that day full of excitement about the future and now here I was, back for another surgery. Another surgery I was sure was a result of the forceps that had been used to deliver my little boy. The forceps I had read did terrible things to women and babies.

I had wondered a few times what would happen if men were the ones who gave birth? I'd bet those things would have been banned years ago. Both of my babies had needed assistance to get them out, but Rose had been delivered using vacuum suction and, to this day, I was confused as to why that option wasn't given to me for Max's birth. Or indeed, why I hadn't been given the cesarean I had asked about several times during my pregnancy. I wished so desperately that I had stuck to my guns and demanded to birth my baby the way I had wanted, instead of allowing those doctors to bully me.

As I sat there in the admissions area my thoughts were interrupted by a young, thin woman calling my name. She was so quiet that I almost missed it. I was led through to a room where I was told to get changed into a gown and socks. A nurse then came in and covered me in one of those wonderful heated blankets. It was still cold, almost unheard of for mid-November, so the warm blanket felt like heaven.

Several people came to see me over the course of the next couple of hours, all of whom asked me the same basic questions. One nurse took my blood pressure, another took my history and told me that I was next on the list. I can't tell you how many times I thought about packing up my stuff and running out of

                    But baby, you're worth it!

there. I was so sure that going ahead with the surgery was a bad idea. But Mum hadn't had an attack since starting the new medication almost a week before. I knew this was the only time I'd ever be able to take nine weeks to recover. I stayed because I wanted to get myself sorted out and better, once and for all. I felt like the antidepressants were starting to work and for the first time in months the cloud was starting to lift. I was starting to see a future again. A future where my little family would be happy and healthy, after all, wasn't that all that really mattered?

Finally, after almost two-and-a-half hours, Dr Anderson came in to see me. We went through what I was having done, my prolapsed uterus would be lifted back up and sewn on both sides to the supporting ligaments. The front and back walls of my vagina would be repaired and the bowel and bladder would be lifted back and secured back into place. I'd mentioned the discharge that I'd told him about when I'd seen him in his rooms back in September and asked him to check that as well. No trouble at all, he informed me that he would need to work both laparoscopically and through the vagina and so would be able to perform a D&C without any issue.

Soon after Dr Anderson's visit I was ready to be wheeled through to theatre. I was pleasantly surprised to see the same guy who had wheeled me through last time —and I wasn't disappointed. Every staff member we passed on the trip up to the operating theatre talked and laughed with my driver. My first thought once again was that this guy was absolutely wasting his wonderful energy in the dingy corridors of this hospital. I soon remembered, though, that he would cheer up the most scared, hopeless patients. I could not imagine anyone being immune to his infectious personality. I only wish I'd caught his name so I could have sent him a thank you card and maybe a gift.

By the time I was wheeled into the anesthetic bay, I was feeling at ease. I was ready to get myself sorted so I could move on with my life. I could get back to looking after my family and, most of all, I could get back to enjoying my babies. I missed them so much already, but I knew I was doing the right thing. Everything would be okay once the operation was done.

Two hours later I was in recovery. I felt like I'd just slept for eight hours, it was lovely. Nurses came to check on me, as did Dr Anderson. The operation had gone well and he expected me to have a good result. He reiterated that I wasn't to lift for six weeks, nor was I to have sex. It was obvious he'd forgotten that I was a single mum with a six-month-old, and I laughed at the thought. I was still feeling pretty groggy but I was keen to get my hands on my phone so I could check in to make sure everyone was okay.

I must have dozed off then because the next thing I knew, I was in the room where I was going to be spending the night. When I had woken up in recovery there hadn't been any pain but by then I was feeling more than a little bit uncomfortable. I had what felt like moderate period pain but it was definitely getting worse. The next time one of the nurses came in, a guy of about 30 with black hair, I asked him if there was anything I could get for the pain. Maybe 20 minutes later he returned with something. I have no idea what that nurse gave me but

     But baby, you're worth it!

it may as well have been a couple of M&Ms for all the good they did.

By 9pm the pain had become unbearable. I had been out of recovery for a couple of hours and I wasn't sure how I was going to make it through the night. Suddenly, I had what felt like an urge to do a poo. I felt like doing so might get rid of the pain. The guy who'd given me the useless painkillers and a couple of female nurses were in the room with me. The guy told me that I was not allowed to stand up until the following day but I couldn't hold it. He actually offered me an adult diaper or a bed pan, I was appalled at the idea of using either of those.

Eventually, I was helped off the bed and into my private bathroom. Someone mentioned the blood, it was everywhere, all over the floor and the bed. I stayed in the bathroom for a minute or two but soon realised that the pain was coming from the front, as well as the rear. What the hell was going on?

Finally, I was all cleaned up and back in bed. I was given more pain relief but once again they may as well have been chocolates because once again, they did nothing, although in fairness they were obviously stronger than the last lot, since they made me feel sick. Thankfully, I was given something for the nausea which did work. I'm not one to cry at the drop of a hat, I'm actually pretty bloody tough, if I do say so myself. But I was in so much pain, more pain than I'd been in with my first labour. When I had begged for that epidural for so many hours after needing to be induced. It was horrific. I genuinely thought at the time that I might die from it. I buzzed the nurses — I needed something to actually ease the pain. I was lying there squirming and crying from it.

The male nurse from earlier came in again, he had the absolute nerve to tell me that I must have a low pain tolerance. I wished at that moment that I could kick him. Who the hell did the guy think he was, making a comment like that to a woman who had just had three internal organs sewn back into place after they had been almost falling out of her body? I only hoped that the look on my face reflected even a fraction of the fury I felt at that moment. I was shocked and angry. And hurt. Later, the fact he left a chocolate bar for the morning nurses to pass on to me made me think that perhaps he'd felt bad about his insensitive comment at least.

After what felt like hours, but was probably a matter of minutes, a wonderful young nurse came in and saw how much pain I was in. She was onto it straight away. I'm not sure what she gave me, but at 2am I finally managed to fall asleep, completely free of pain. I managed to sleep for about five hours before I had a room full of people bustling about for the morning shift change.

The following morning was a blur, I had lovely women looking after me. One of them was quite young, and she was fascinated by the fact I'd chosen to go it solo from the word go to have my second baby. This was something she had thought about as well, but she didn't know anyone who'd actually done it. Another of the nurses was around my age and she had decided to retrain and study nursing now that her kids were at university. She was still learning and so had a more senior nurse with her when

     But baby, you're worth it!

she was actually performing her duties, but she came in several times just to check in. I felt a bit vindicated by the reactions of those nurses when I had explained why I had needed this operation. They were both suitably horrified.

I'd had the same reaction from my brothers, my sister-in-law and my few close friends that I had told about the ordeal, including my friend Theo. Theo had a heart of gold. We'd met in our early 20's and had dated for a while, but it hadn't lasted for long, eventually we drifted apart and lost touch. Some 20 years later I had looked him up because I was curious to know what had become of him. When we had known each other all those years ago, he had been a tech nerd who lived in Bondi. Now he was doing freelance photography, mostly wildlife stuff, and conservation work up in Coffs Harbour.

I don't really have male friends, not the kind that I would tell something so personal to anyway. Theo was the one exception; he was the guy I could tell anything to. We had history and trust. My wonderful friend Theo wanted to see someone pay for what had happened to me. I was starting to realise that it really wasn't okay, what had happened to me was not normal and it was not okay. It wasn't just the people who loved and cared about me that were shocked and outraged, it was medical professionals too.

By lunchtime I started to suspect that I wasn't going to be allowed to go home. I was still bleeding fairly heavily, certainly more than the doctor would have liked. There was talk about low ferritin levels, and I didn't need to be told what that meant as I'd needed two iron infusions while I was pregnant. The doctor came in to see me not long after the plate of inedible lunch slop was removed from my tray table. As it turned out, the nurses had a stash of sandwiches to hand out to anyone who couldn't eat the atrocious food. Thank goodness because a 50g chocolate bar can only stretch so far! Dr Anderson asked me if I could recall the conversation we'd had the previous day, as it turned out I couldn't at all. It was frustrating and a little embarrassing, but he assured me that it was completely normal to have forgotten a conversation that had taken place so soon after an anesthetic.

We went through what had happened and indeed what been discovered during the operation: The last doctor had not cleaned all of the debris out of my uterus. Six months after giving birth to my little boy there were still products of conception. It suddenly made sense why that last doctor had been so blasé about my prolapse. He had actually tried to insist on assisting with the surgery, I had found out when we had finally secured a date. Finding out that he had left debris behind suddenly explained why he had wanted to assist. I was so glad I'd shut that down. As soon as I found out about that I had asked for another doctor, because the guy made me feel uncomfortable. Thankfully, Dr Anderson had absolutely no issue with doing whatever I was comfortable with. I was so thankful at that moment that I'd had a decent and caring doctor for my surgery.

Unfortunately, my fears were not unfounded, I was going to have to stay in hospital for another night. I was still bleeding too much, they needed to check my iron levels again in the morning

But baby, you're worth it!

and then I'd have the gauze inside of me removed. Apparently, the latter was not going to be fun... I realised that I really was going to have to make that chocolate bar last as long as possible.

Every couple of hours I checked in with Mum, Nick and my babies. Max was used to talking to Ally on FaceTime when she would call mum, but he had never seen his mummy in the phone before and he was amused. Thank goodness Mum had been with him daily from the moment he was born. It made it so much easier being away from him knowing my mum had such a special bond with him, just as she did with Rose. It probably sounds selfish but I was also a bit jealous. I believed with all my might that Max actually saw Mum as his main parental figure. I felt like my bond with him wasn't as strong. It broke my heart more than just a little bit.

Everyone was okay. Thankfully, Mum hadn't had an attack. Rose was helping like the wonderful kid she always was. Nick was using my office for a few hours and just really enjoying spending some time with the girls and his new little mate. They had also received a care package that day, it was addressed to me. Geri, the mum who'd been such a wonderful help at Rose's party had sent a weeks' worth of meals, and some desserts to make sure that everyone was fed. We were all so grateful to this beautiful woman, her gesture of kindness was something none of us would ever forget.

Finally, it was time to let Mum and the babies get sorted for bed. Nick was staying downstairs and looking forward to trying out the new recliner sofa I'd recently bought. A couple of hours later I was given the same pain relief that had worked to knock me out in the early hours of the morning. But unlike the day before, they made me feel like throwing up. The nurse told me that in order to get rid of the horrible nausea she'd have to give me something to knock me out.

"Bring it on," I said to her. That was at 10pm, the next thing I knew it was 7am the next morning. It was the first time I'd slept nine hours since Max had arrived back in May. I was feeling on top of the world. Well, the bar was pretty low at that point, but things were looking up.

But baby, you're worth it!

Chapter 19

Tuesday, 15th Nov — Continued

Once again, I woke to the sound of the nurses walking into my room for their shift change. The last day-and-a-half had dragged on forever, but I was going home later that day. I was going to finally get back to my beautiful babies, I could not wait! By 9am I'd had my wounds re-dressed and the horrible cannula removed from my left wrist. I was ready to go. I'd also had the gauze taken out that had been inserted during surgery. Dr Anderson had warned me that it would not be pleasant — what an understatement that was. There wasn't any pain as such, just a bit of discomfort but, holy hell, it was like watching that magic trick where the clown pulls coloured handkerchiefs, all tied together, out of their sleeves. But it was being pulled out of me, and it was the longest magic trick I'd ever witnessed, it took so long that I was starting to feel the anticipation in the air. I think the nurses were becoming as embarrassed as I was. It really seemed like it would never end. It was more than a little awkward.

As it turned out I had lost a lot of blood, more than normal for the operation I'd had. A repeat blood test earlier that morning had shown that my iron levels were extremely low. I would need an iron infusion. A new cannula would need to be inserted, what a horrible thought, but necessary. I had gone weeks before I was given the first iron infusion during my pregnancy. One of the doctors at the ante-natal clinic seemed to think I should have just sucked it up. It had been horrible. The fatigue was like nothing I'd ever experienced. I'd sleep nine hours and wake up feeling like I hadn't slept in a month. I was grateful that I wouldn't be going through that again. A new needle in my hand was a small price to pay to get it sorted out before I went home.

By 11am the iron infusion had been done and I was free to go. Nick was coming to pick me up, I just had to make a quick trip to the hospital pharmacy to pick up some pain medication. I was sure I wouldn't need such strong painkillers but decided I should still grab them, just in case. By the time I had made it down to the pharmacy I could barely walk or even stand. I was genuinely shocked by how much pain I was in, I thought that I was over the pain but it was back. I couldn't understand why I had a heaviness and excruciating pain in my groin. It didn't make sense.

After picking up my medication I began to make my way slowly towards the doors that lead out to the patient pick up area. I looked up to see Nick hurrying towards me. A huge rush of relief washed over me, it had been a rough couple of days, far more so than I had been expecting and I was so happy to see my little brother. I was so glad to be going home, to finally have the last hurdle behind me. I was ready to get home and get on with my life. I just wished that I wasn't in so much bloody pain.

          But baby, you're worth it!

Ten minutes later, we were home. I was so grateful to Nick for looking after Mum and the kids while I was gone. I kissed my babies a million and one times. I'd missed their sweet faces so much. But I was shocked to find that I was scared to hold my little Max. I was so desperate to cuddle my baby but the pain was even worse than what I had experienced in those first weeks after his birth. It didn't make sense! Surely, the pain should be in my stomach, where everything had been lifted and sewn back onto the ligaments. But the pain wasn't in my stomach, it was down lower. It felt like I'd given birth all over again, but so much worse. How was this possible? I didn't understand. I'd had the D&C, and my vagina had been repaired, whatever that meant, but there shouldn't have been anything like that level of pain, should there?

The next few days were a blur. I could not for the life of me understand why the pain was not getting any better. I was getting more and more frustrated. I was supposed to be getting better but instead I could barely sit, and when I did, I couldn't sit straight, only on my side, if that makes sense? I couldn't wash dishes, or fix Rose a sandwich. I could barely shower let alone give my little boy a bath. I had been prepared for the fact that I wouldn't be able to pick my baby up but nothing could have prepared me for the fact that I could not hold him, bathe or even cuddle him.

Max was still sleeping in the bassinet that Mum had set up for him upstairs. He'd slept in it a couple of times after a sleepless night here and there, but he was supposed to sleep downstairs in his cot once I got home, he was supposed to be with his mummy. I was so grateful to Mum for holding the fort, but I felt like I was losing my baby, or that I was losing my bond with him anyway. The operation was not supposed to make things worse. What was going on?

The first weekend after the surgery, I had organised for a lady to come and pick up an inflatable kayak I'd sold her online. I had purchased it during the Covid lockdowns, with the intention of taking Rose out on the harbour near home. We had hardshell kayaks but they were too heavy to lift by myself so the inflatable tandem kayak was going to be the perfect solution. Of course, more than two years later it was still sitting in the box, gathering dust, so I was happy to free up the space. Plus, I hadn't worked for three months so I was ever conscious of my dwindling funds.

The lady arrived right at the allocated time but she was only tiny and she hadn't brought anyone with her. I apologised and explained that I wasn't going to be able to help her lift the kayak as I'd had an operation a few days before. She asked if I was okay, and, of course that set me off. I burst into tears and told her what I'd just had done. I'm not sure what made me blurt out my story to a total stranger, I felt instantly at ease with the tiny lady with the English accent.

It turned out that she had had a similar experience with a forceps delivery over 40 years earlier when she had given birth to her son. I was shocked to hear that she had been living with the same issues. The incontinence, the pain and tenderness. She had learned to live with those awful problems but had

     But baby, you're worth it!

decided to either have the repair or a hysterectomy finally. She was planning to have surgery the following year. I told her to do her proper research before deciding on the surgery, I had found out too late exactly what the repair surgery entailed, and I would hate to see another woman go through the same thing without fully understanding what she was in for. Eventually she left, happy with her purchase.

I felt a tiny shift after that chance encounter. Up until that point, I had never heard firsthand from another woman who had suffered from such a traumatic birth injury. I had several close friends who had given birth naturally and several who had had cesarean births. I couldn't say for sure, but I didn't think that any of the women who'd delivered naturally had ever been through anything quite as terrible as what I had.

One of my school friends had had a hysterectomy a few years earlier, although it was not related to birth injuries. I could not believe that one of my dearest friends had been through such a horrible operation and recovery and I had done nothing to help her. I couldn't even articulate how sad and regretful that made me. To think I hadn't done anything more than send my get well wishes.

I had been determined not to take the strong pain killers that I'd brought home from the hospital but by day two I conceded that I was going to have to take a couple. I knew the tablets made you a little bit out of it and so I waited until Rose was in bed before grabbing a couple. I sat down carefully and reclined my side of the lounge. I'd put half a dozen of my favorite Christmas lollies in a cup and within 20 minutes I was absolutely, blissfully removed from reality.

Very quickly my night-time habit became my escape from the fresh new hell that I was living. I discovered, a couple of days after coming home from the hospital, that "vaginal repairs" actually involved cutting all the way up the front and back walls of the vagina and then sewing them back together. I had felt the stitches while in the toilet and then madly searched the internet for answers about why they were there. Oh my gosh, what had I done?

I had done my research: how did I not know that the operation would involve cutting and sewing me back together like that? How had I gone through with such a major operation without doing my own due diligence and researching it properly? It also occurred to me that the way I'd been sewn back together would surely make it impossible to ever have sex again. Sure, at that moment it was the furthest thing from my mind. But one day my kids would be older, and I was certain that my prince charming was out there somewhere but what was the point in hoping that I would find him, when I would no longer be able to enjoy the things that other consenting adults did?

It was bad enough that my lovely knickers had been replaced by those horrid big black grandma undies I'd had to wear for months. Actually, I'd seen my Mum's undies on the washing lines enough times to know that, although they weren't the G-strings I'd been happily wearing since my teens, Mum's knickers were nothing as terrible as the bloody parachutes I'd been wearing

          But baby, you're worth it!

for over six months. All because I was still wearing maternity pads.

I had done some pretty stupid things in my life. I had dated totally unsuitable guys, I was an absolute horror of a teenager. My father had been a horrible man who had terrorised my family. Michael had always wanted his validation but Nick and I were terrified of him. The day my mum finally kicked him out, when I was 14, had been one of the happiest days of my childhood. I had been too scared to look at him, let alone talk, for fear that I'd be screamed at or smacked. So, at 14 I suddenly found myself, for the first time ever, free.

I was free to talk, free to say no, free to have friends over without being screamed at and ridiculed in front of them. I was even allowed to cry without being told to shut up. So, I did what seemed justified at the time. I took my newfound freedom and I ran with it. I rebelled, and I rebelled hard. I was a nightmare, I went from being the sweet, quiet and agreeable girl to the loud, unreasonable little monster. Mum had often joked that I grew horns overnight, and I wouldn't disagree. I had never regretted anything more than putting my mum through hell in those teenage years. Until then. I was starting to really regret my decision to go ahead with the surgery.

A week or so after the surgery I started bleeding much more heavily than before. Dr Anderson suspected I had an infection, so I was put on a 10-day course of antibiotics. I was living an absolute nightmare. I still couldn't even cuddle my sweet little boy. I missed him so much. I missed the way he would grab my face with his chubby little hands and attack my chin with his gummy little mouth. I was so desperate to have him back in his cot, but more importantly, to have him back in my arms.

I stopped taking the pain killers that I'd been given at the hospital. Even though they were the only thing that actually got rid of the pain, I realised after a few nights that I was moving into dangerous territory. Those things ruined people's lives. I was really enjoying the feelings of happiness and elation after I had taken them, but I could see how people developed an addiction to them as well. So, I put a stop to my little night-time habit, before it became one.

On a positive note, Mum was doing much better than she had been for weeks. She had only needed one injection in the past couple of weeks, because she'd been out in the hot sun working. I'd had a bit of a meltdown at the time, I was terrified of having Mum sick and somehow having to pick up the slack, at least for the time being. Thankfully, at least so far, the new medication she was taking seemed to be working.

I was still in so much pain and thoroughly regretting the decision to have the surgery, but I was slowly starting to feel a bit better. I'd had the wonderful meals sent by Geri while I was in hospital. I also had a beautiful bunch of flowers waiting from Nick when I got home. Tina had popped over one day with some beautiful flowers and a meal as well. My school friends and Chelsea and Lindsay had all sent flowers. Even my friends at Attimo had delivered half a dozen meals for us, even though it had been a Saturday, their busiest day of the week.

I hadn't actually told many people about the operation, and no one knew quite the extent of what I had been through over those months since Max was born, so to have so much love sent my way really helped while I went through that hell. It helped to set me on what felt was at least the beginning of my healing journey.

Max had been an absolute champion sleeper while I was in hospital and for the first week or so that I was home. It helped to ease my guilt about leaving Mum to look after him through the night. But then, a week later, so around the time that I was just starting to feel a bit better, Mum admitted that the poor little fellow hadn't been sleeping very well. He still didn't have any teeth at just a couple of weeks shy of seven months and you could see the bulge on his bottom gums, so it was easy to figure out what was going on.

My boy had been waking every hour or so, meaning that Mum had been getting up to rock him back to sleep, getting no more than a couple of hours sleep for herself. I knew that wasn't sustainable, I knew that it was time to take Max back downstairs and pop him in my bed for a while. I had co-slept with Rose until she was about the same age. It was no brainer. I could do so safely with my bed against the wall on one side and Max's cot pushed up against the other side. Mum wasn't keen on this plan but she was completely exhausted, so she gave in.

Rose and I were excited about having our baby back downstairs, we had both missed him so much. But I was more than a little nervous as well. Max had become so attached to Mum that

I was worried he would cry for her. I was relieved that, although he did stir a fair amount through the night, I was able to give him his dummy and each time he went straight back to sleep. Rose and I had a few evening functions over the following couple of weeks for her year six graduation, and so I was relieved to know that everybody would at least be well rested for those events.

Chapter 20
Thursday,
8th December, 2022

On Thursday, just three weeks, and two days after my operation, I put on a lovely dress and some ridiculously high wedge sandals, and headed over to the concert hall where Rose's end-of-year performance was to be held. I felt like a bit of a fraud, walking around the forecourt and talking to other parents and teachers. To everyone else I suppose I looked the same, but underneath that pink dress, my body was far from okay. My mind was starting to heal though, and I knew that this was a big step in the right direction.

The following week we had functions almost every day, a graduation dinner and ceremony, a pool party for the kids to jump into Geri's pool with their uniforms on, and then a picnic from lunchtime on the last day of school. It was exhausting, but we did it. I even managed to have a glass of bubbly and a dance at the dinner.

Nothing in the world could made me happier, add to that the knowledge that my beautiful eldest child had such a wonderful end to her primary school career. She had made lifelong friends and been blessed with the most amazing teacher that any parent could ever wish for. My body was still a long way from being okay but my head was back in the game, and my heart was bursting.

By the time school finished for the year, a month had passed since my prolapse surgery. By that point I was feeling less pain. I had, however, started to suspect that the prolapse had at least partially come back. The familiar heaviness in my groin had returned, but Christmas was less than two weeks away. I was able to sit more comfortably. I could do the dishes without having to take breaks. I could go to the supermarket and even drive myself there and, of course, I could cuddle my sweet baby. None of those things had been possible three weeks earlier. It had been a tough time but I'd come out the other end, at least for the most part.

My follow-up with Dr Anderson was scheduled just a few days before Christmas. I wasn't expecting great news. Once again, I knew my own body. I knew where everything was supposed to go and so I was preparing myself for the probability that the surgery hadn't completely fixed my injuries. I had made the decision, however, that no matter what the outcome of that next appointment was, I was not having any more surgeries. At least not while my children were so young.

Thankfully the incontinence had mostly sorted itself out. I still couldn't walk long distances and I looked like an absolute goose the one time, in a mad panic to get to school in time, that I had

   But baby, you're worth it!

tried to run. There was absolutely no way I would be going another day without being able to cuddle my Max. Whatever the outcome of my surgery was, I was going to learn to live with it.

Sweet little Max was seven months old. He finally cut those first two cute baby teeth a couple of days before he turned seven months. Almost the same time as Rose sprouted her first two teeth all those years ago. There was only about a day or two in it. My little boy really was still such a baby. Rose had been an overachiever. She was rolling at four months. Sitting at six months and then at seven-and-a-half months. I remember taking great pleasure in her ability to crawl over to the sofa, pull herself up and then walk along holding onto the edge. I loved every moment of her clever achievement.

Max was nowhere near ready to get up and walk, nor did I expect him to crawl any time soon. He could sit up, but as soon as an object was placed within his field of vision, he would lunge himself towards it and end up on his tummy. There were no words yet, either. Rose was making mama and nanna sounds by that time, but not Max. He certainly had a lot to say, it was hilarious and gorgeous, the baby babbling. Max had the funniest little deep voice; it was the complete opposite of Rose and her little pipsqueak voice. I had forgotten how sweet the sound of your baby's voice was. It really was what I needed. I had felt so much despair about the months where I was too sick and in too much pain to enjoy my baby. It felt like I had missed out on so much, it was like he knew that I was okay now but that I needed him to stay a little baby for a bit longer, now that I could just revel in his sweet, tiny perfection.

Chapter 21
Friday, 9th December, 2022

n the madness of the end-of-school concert day I had missed a call from the law firm I had been in touch with. I hadn't spoken with them in weeks. I had, however, shared the doctor's report from the prolapse surgery. I had also shared what Dr Anderson had told me when he came to visit me on the morning following the surgery — when I had been told that the prolapse was absolutely caused by the forceps, and the retained placenta, and weeks of infection, would likely have contributed as well. I knew I had a strong case. I had two fertility specialists who I'd seen in the couple of years leading up to the birth of my little boy, and both of those doctors would be able to confirm there were no previous issues that could possibly have contributed to such a severe prolapse of not just my uterus but the neighbouring organs.

I had learned that pelvic organ prolapse was a risk associated with a forceps delivery, but of course nobody had told me that at the time. I should have been offered the option of a vacuum delivery, or a cesarean. I also should never have been cut to the degree that I was, and then there was the whole placenta and infection debacle.

But baby, you're worth it!

I enjoyed the school concert thoroughly, especially when my girl was on stage. Rose had given orders on where Brittany and I should sit. I would never, ever tire of seeing my sweet girl, who was one growth spurt away from overtaking her nanna in height, on the stage.

I was looking forward to speaking with the lawyer the following morning and so made sure that I had everyone fed and cleaned up and by 9am. Rose had gone with Mum to school and Max was getting grumbly as it was time for his morning nap. I called quickly to check in and see what the lawyers needed, I figured it would only be a quick call. It was strange that they were calling now. After all, I hadn't had my follow-up appointment yet, so I had nothing new to report. Oh well, I thought to myself, I'd wait and see what they needed. No one answered though, so I left a message and then got Max sorted for his nap.

Max slept until about 11:20am, I had just changed him and was playing with him on the rug while I waited for his bottle to heat up. Suddenly my phone rang. I recognised the phone number as that of the law firm and so I answered. The caller was indeed the lawyer that I had spoken with at length when my prolapse had been discovered all those weeks earlier. Pleasantries were exchanged, she was glad to hear that I had been starting to feel better.

Next up, I wanted to confirm that she had received my last couple of emails, which she had. I reminded this woman that I had not yet had my follow-up appointment, just in case she was calling to see how things had gone, but it was fine, she was aware of that. She asked a couple of questions about whether I was given an episiotomy before the forceps had been used. Yes I said, I'd ended up tearing as well, I explained that the degree of the cut was apparently the likely cause of the loss of control of my bladder and bowels, at least in those early weeks.

By then I had taken Max's bottle out of the warmer and was feeding him. I had figured out a way to get him safely onto the lounge without lifting him. I'd had my phone on speaker since answering the call so I could have my hands free to tend to my little boy.

What came next made me glad that I wasn't holding my phone, as I'm sure I would have dropped it. I was informed that because the episiotomy had been performed before the forceps were used to pull my baby out, it would be impossible to put a case together. The woman explained that nothing else that had happened would be worth building a case on either.

Not even the fact that the injuries and subsequent repairs had left me unable to have another baby. A fact that had been eating away at me for months and was the reason I was going to have to somehow navigate the whole complicated world of surrogacy in order to have my third precious baby.

I had hoped that when the surgery was completed, I would be able to have my last baby, and that, somehow, I had misunderstood what I had been told previously by Doctor Anderson — but I had heard it loud and clear. Dr Anderson had once again confirmed there was no way I could carry a

                    But baby, you're worth it!

baby without my uterus falling out of my body, which would be catastrophic for both me and my baby.

None of it mattered at that moment. I realised there was no point in continuing the conversation. I thanked the woman for her time. For some reason she decided at that moment to ask another question, but I stopped her, what was the point? She had made it clear that injuries like mine came with the territory. I was told that allowing the doctor, who was supposed to do no harm, to deliver my baby with forceps meant that I basically should have expected those injuries, that it was my own fault for allowing it.

I had been told by Dr Anderson, the doctor who had repaired the terrible damage done by those forceps, that my injuries were not normal and that it was not okay. How could that woman tell me that I needed to just suck it up? She wasn't a doctor, and she hadn't consulted with an independent medical professional as she had promised me that she would do. I was absolutely gob-smacked. You could have knocked me down with a feather. I could not listen to her offensive crap any longer. I thanked her for her time once again. Thanks for nothing I thought, as I hung up, barely holding back my tears.

I somehow managed to hold back those tears until after I hung up. I felt absolutely gutted. I felt like someone had ripped my heart out of my chest, I felt lower than I had done in months. Mum happened to pop her head into my kitchen about 5 minutes after I had ended the call. I was sobbing. Big, ugly, mascara-smudging sobs. I had been so determined to get those doctors to pay for what they had done. It wasn't even about the money, although it would have been nice to recoup even some of the thousands of dollars I'd spent on operations, scans and medications since Max's birth. However, justice is what I really wanted. And an apology would have been nice.

Nothing could give me back the precious time I had lost with my baby. When I'd been in too much pain to care for him. The months of pain and mental anguish. My daughter had had to watch her healthy and capable mother turn into an invalid. Mum had ended up losing her own health in the process of having to suddenly care for her adult daughter and newborn baby. None of it should have happened. How could that ignorant woman so callously tell me that it was all okay and it was basically my own fault?

I had come so far in the previous couple of weeks. I'd been starting to feel positive and happy again for the first time in months. I had really enjoyed the end of year concert and had been so looking forward to the graduation dinner the following week. I had talked excitedly with a couple of the other mums and was planning to have a little boogie and a glass of wine. I was starting to look forward to the future again, to my baby boy's first Christmas, and Rose's last one before she became a teenager. We had holidays, Easter and two very special birthdays to look forward to the following year. I needed to be strong. Somehow, I had to overcome this latest hurdle. I had to rally, for Rose, for Max and for my mum.

But baby, you're worth it!

Chapter 22
Sunday, 11th December, 2022

One thing I realised at that moment was that I had struggled silently through the whole ordeal. I had been too proud and embarrassed to talk about what had happened, and what I'd been through. Sure, I had shared some of it with a few very close friends, but I was far too proud to admit that I needed help. My father had been in the army and from a young age I was taught that weakness of any sort was a character flaw. I had taken that advice to heart as I grew into adulthood and, as a result, I had always found it to be a sign of weakness to admit to anyone that I needed help. I preferred to focus my energy instead on keeping everyone else happy. The lady who had bought the kayak a few days after my surgery was the only person, apart from my mum and the medical professionals, that I'd told the full horrible story to. With the exception of that lawyer.

I realised then what I needed to do. I needed to do what a counselor had advised me to do years before, when I had tried to understand what had driven my father in his hatred towards his young children, and his wife. I had been desperate to understand what we had done to cause his anger and nastiness.

But that wasn't how it worked, there was no way anyone else could give me those answers.

I had been given a couple of options to help me try to heal from the trauma of a childhood spent tiptoeing around him. I could talk to him, ask him the questions that I so desperately wanted answers to. That wasn't an option, even then as a young adult, I was still far too scared of him to ask the questions I craved answers for. I'd never had a normal conversation with my father so I wouldn't have even known where to start.

The other option had been to write a letter. It was a common therapeutic technique to help people to heal from trauma, especially when that trauma had been caused by the actions of another person. I had written my father a letter, it had taken me a few days. I had poured my heart out. I had told him how his actions had affected me and how they'd affected my brothers, and my mum. And when it was finished, I felt free. The counselor had been right. Pouring my thoughts and feelings out onto paper had healed me.

That must have been 25 years ago. I saw my father once, a couple of years later, at his request. I sat at the table that day and watched as he abused and dismissed his new wife and my brother every time one of them opened their mouths. I stayed silent and simply observed. I had been told that he had changed, that he wanted to make an effort to get to know his children now that we were adults. He hadn't changed, but on that day, I knew that the letter I had written a couple of years earlier really had healed me.

But baby, you're worth it!

I was no longer scared of him. He hadn't changed and that lunch allowed me to finally see him for what he was. A big, fat bully. I walked away that day with a spring in my step. I never saw him again and I doubt that I ever will again. He will never see the letter, in fact I burned it. I had written it for myself and burning it had freed me. I had poured out onto those pages all of the trauma and grief I'd held onto from a childhood spent terrified of that man,.

I had always considered myself to be a fairly articulate person, I knew I could tell my story. I wasn't sure where to start or how to frame it but I knew that writing my story would help me continue to heal from all the trauma, and from this latest setback. So, I took little Max outside in his pram and decided to write a post on one of my social media pages. I told everyone that I wanted to talk about the injuries I had sustained from the use of forceps and the terrible impact that it had had on my life, and the lives of those closest to me. I was absolutely terrified, I had no idea if people would be supportive or if they'd think it was a massive faux pas, a case of TMI (too much information). There was only one way to find out.

Within a couple of hours of writing the first post, I was overwhelmed with support from friends, both here and overseas. I received messages from two beautiful women I knew, telling me they couldn't wait to read about my story. Both of them had sustained terrible injuries because of forceps deliveries. One of the women had ongoing problems, even though her daughter was almost 19. The other was my friend Chelsea's good friend from school, who I had also known for many years. She'd had such a traumatic birth with her daughter that she had been terrified about giving birth again. When her son came along a few years later she needed to have a cesarean to ensure her injuries from the forceps did not become any worse.

I was floored. I had been going through absolute hell for months, thinking that it was just me. I was just unlucky; the forceps hadn't been used properly. That's what I had assumed through those dark and lonely months. But I was starting to realise my experience might not be that unique, after all. As I started to ask questions in a couple of pregnancy forums, I was sad, and angry, to read the responses from women who had sustained life changing injuries because of the use of forceps, just like I had.

Why did no one talk about their experiences? Of course, I knew exactly why. It's not ladylike to talk about your genitals. It definitely wasn't okay to talk about childbirth, in case you scared or triggered other women. I understood the logic, but what about those of us who were suffering in silence?

We don't talk about the dark truth, the reality that is childbirth for a lot of women. We don't want to seem ungrateful. There are women who would love to be going through whatever was thrown at them, just for the opportunity to hold their babies in their arms. I totally understood that rationale.

I had been to the ends of the earth to have my little boy, thinking I would never see the day that I would welcome my second child into the world. But then when I had, it was the start of a

But baby, you're worth it!

nightmare. It wasn't my baby's fault, and it sure as hell wasn't mine, despite what that lawyer said, nor the doctor who did my first surgery, who'd had the nerve to joke about my condition.

I hadn't signed up for life-altering injuries, ones that prevented me from having more children, prevented me from holding my own children for months and destroyed my mental health — at least for a time until I had been forced to take medication to get my mind out of the dark place it had been headed in. No one should be forced to endure what I had. This was Australia, we had one of the best health systems in the world, and yet there I was suffering from horrific but totally avoidable injuries. And I wasn't the only one.

So, that weekend I started writing. I started to put the words down on paper, well on my phone, that's how I started. I began writing my experience down in the notes section on my phone, while my baby boy slept peacefully against my chest. I never intended to write a book. I wanted to start a blog and share snippets of my story with the world, to help myself recover and to help other women to understand that they were not alone. But I found myself sharing the story, sharing so much of my story, in order to paint the picture of how my injuries had affected my life, and the lives of the people closest to me.

Chapter 23
Sunday, 25th December, 2022

The week or so before Christmas was a busy one. The weekend after school had wrapped up, I had gotten a bit carried away on the website of one of my favourite retailers. I had a voucher from Dani to spend and here was a huge sale on kids' fashion according to the website I had landed on via a google search. So I decided to buy a few dresses each for Rose and Ally. I found a couple of lovely tops for Mum and myself as well so I happily purchased them all.

I was so excited about Christmas that I hadn't thought anything about the fact there was nowhere to enter the code from the voucher Dani had given me for my birthday. It wasn't until the following Monday that I realised the confirmation email looked suspicious. Sure enough, my bank statement confirmed it. I had been shopping on a fake, scam website. Of course, I was disappointed but thankful I had only lost a little over $100.

I'd been on that website for some retail therapy because I had decided to splurge to make myself feel better about the terrible haircut I'd ended up with the week before. I had been living with that weird post pregnancy hair that motivates so many

                    But baby, you're worth it!

women to get the chop. It was the day of Rose's graduation mass and so I had decided to go and get a couple of inches cut off with some layering. I loved my long blonde hair, but it had been desperately in need of a tidy up for months. I had decided that I deserved a pamper so I made an appointment at a salon near Rose's school that I had never been to before.

Unfortunately, by the time I realised the woman had cut about eight inches off my hair it was too late. I sat there for the next 15 minutes, watching on in horror as the woman gave me what I can only describe as a lady mullet! I actually realised when I got home that I'd been given a weird little rat's tail as well so ended up having to cut that off myself.

At first, I was horrified I would have to go out with a weird lady mullet, but it wasn't the end of the world. I knew that the disgusting haircut would have absolutely tipped me over the edge a few weeks earlier. Instead of letting it destroy my happiness, I simply dyed it a cute pastel shade of pink. Summer was too hot to wear my hair out anyway, so I was going to have a cute pink ponytail for a while. And wouldn't you know it, the bank was able to recoup the money from my shopping misadventure as well.

Mum and I made the decision to postpone the trip to Florida again. We had been planning to re-schedule it for the April holidays but, although I was starting to take Max out more and more, there was no way I was ready to take him to another country. What if he became sick or injured? Never mind the fact that we would be stopping over in LAX. I had been through that airport enough times to know that I had no interest in doing it with an 11-month-old baby.

Instead of the US trip we made the decision to head up to the Gold Coast, an hour away by plane. We arranged to fly up there for a week and stay with Mum's best friend Robin. Robin and her sister, niece and nephew lived in a huge home just minutes from Mermaid Beach. We had stayed with them early in my pregnancy, just a week after I'd had that terrifying bleed. It was strange to think about how much had happened since then. Everyone was looking forward to catching up and it would be a great way to test Max on a plane. If he hated it then at least it was only a short trip.

Christmas time was in full swing and we were living every moment of it to the fullest. If there is one more thing I should have told you about myself, it is that Christmas has always been by far my favourite time of the year.

If it wasn't for Halloween, which had always been quite the occasion in our neighbourhood, I would probably decorate for Christmas in September. Everything about Christmas fills me with joy, especially since I'd had children of my own.

Thankfully, I had ordered most of my Christmas shopping online and wrapped most of it before that last operation, and I'd finished wrapping it during the last week of school. I'd also decorated our carport with all sorts of wonderful new bits and pieces, including a beautiful gold-and-silver wreath made of baubles. Our garden lights never actually come down after

Christmas. What was the rush? They looked so bright and cheerful, after all. I had gone as far as to suggest to Rose that it would be fun to go caroling to try and raise money for a children's charity that we tried to support as often as we could, but apparently the thought was far too embarrassing. Oh well, it had been worth a try, I'd definitely be trying that again the following year, just in case.

The elf had shown up on the 1st of December, as she always does. I both love and hate that thing. I had been a bit worried that she might not get up to mischief this year but she did. She even ordered a box of 12 donuts to be delivered for Rose and her cousins, the cheeky little minx had even used my credit card to pay for them, for the third year in a row! Apparently, we were going to add to the elf family with a boy elf for Max next year. I cringed at the thought, but knew I would be happy seeing the excitement on his sweet little face when the time came.

Before I knew it, it was Christmas Eve and everyone was dressed in their matching pyjamas and ready for bed. Cookies and milk were out for Santa and a carrot had been left for the reindeer. Rose and I were excitedly wondering what Santa would leave for her and Max. Our funny little boy seemed to understand there was something going on, the sweet little fellow. He fought as hard as he could to stay awake but eventually exhaustion won and he drifted off to his dream land.

Christmas morning was wonderful as it always was, and then some. Rose's enthusiasm seemed to have rubbed off on Max. He had opened a present the day before so was well acquainted with wrapping paper, he loved to rip and then eat it. Santa obviously knew that my kids had been good this year as they were both spoilt rotten. There were skateboards, stitch toys, skin care products for Rose and some of the cutest little clothes for Max. He would be the best dressed guy around the following winter, that was for sure.

Mum and Brittany came downstairs at about 7:30am to exchange gifts. Everyone had a wonderful time exchanging gifts and, before I knew it, the time had come for Max to go down for his morning sleep.

By midday Max was up and ready to continue the celebrations. It wasn't long before my brothers, their partners and children arrived ,along with a few other family members. My friend Theo was supposed to come down from Coffs for the week, but I had needed to cancel as I wasn't quite feeling up to having house visitors just yet and so it was a fairly small and intimate affair.

Everyone knew that Mum had been having her Menieres attacks again and so there were lots of helpers on hand to bring the roast dinner down and lay it out on the barbeque table that I had draped a red and white tablecloth over the top off. We're a classy bunch, after all.

Max was happily eating his peanut butter on toast while everyone served themselves lunch. I even managed to get him to try some of Mum's delicious stuffing and some pumpkin. Another milestone, it was the first time my little monkey ate

But baby, you're worth it!

vegetables without gagging. Mum had needed an injection that morning. She hadn't been sure if she was about to have a turn or if she was just panicking but figured it was better to be safe than sorry.

I could see my mother was getting a kick out of how much everyone was enjoying the meal. It was lovely to see her so happy and looking carefree, it had been far too long since I had last seen her that way.

The festivities continued until late afternoon. The girls and Jonathan had a great time with a board game that he had given Rose. I'm not sure what the aim of the game was, but there were 2 foam avocados that were being flung around, much to the delight of the girls who squealed with each direct hit on Jonathan.

Christmas bonbons had been cracked open, paper hats had been worn merrily as bad Christmas jokes were shared around the table. It had been a wonderful day for everyone. I was so happy, and for the first time in such a long time I felt like my family was happy. The tears that stung my eyes at that moment were once again the happy kind. It was pure bliss.

Once everyone had left and the leftovers had been packed away, we sat outside on the patio enjoying the unseasonably cool breeze. We sat and enjoyed reflecting on the day as I fed Max and the girls once again showed us some of their gifts. Everyone had had a lovely Christmas and we'd all been thoroughly spoilt. Before I knew it the kids were bathed and dressed in yet another pair of matching pyjamas they had been given by Santa.

It occurred to me, as it had many times during the day that the following day would be six weeks since the prolapse surgery and the day I was officially allowed to pick up my little boy again. I couldn't help but wonder why, though, was I still bleeding and more than just a bit? And there was still some pain. I'd been too busy over the last couple of weeks to think too much about it.

I had ended up postponing my follow-up appointment with Dr Anderson. I hadn't realised at the time that it had coincided with the Santa photo booking I had made. It had been too late to book another suitable time to get the photos done so I'd had no choice but to push the follow-up out to the new year. There was no way I was missing my children's first Santa photo together. I was hoping the bleeding would start to ease off soon. Surely, it would?

But I stepped away from those thoughts. All that mattered at that moment was that my family had enjoyed a wonderful Christmas. Mum had been fine after the injection and we'd had a magical day just as I had hoped. Once they were in bed Rose and Max both fell asleep quickly, exhausted from their first Christmas together.

I played on my phone for a short while, answering messages from Lindsay and Chelsea in our group chat. We exchanged pictures of all the kids opening their presents that morning and just generally enjoying their day. We also spent some time

　　　　　　　　　　But baby, you're worth it!

chatting about the plans for Lindsay's upcoming baby shower. My friend was going to be having her third baby, but first little girl, in mid-February. We were all so excited.

Both of my friends had had all kinds of struggles bringing their children into the world too and I was so excited to think there was going to be another new baby in just a matter of weeks. I eventually realised how exhausted I was, and so once we had agreed on a few details that needed our attention urgently, I decided it was time for me to get to sleep too. I wished the girls a Merry Christmas, before closing my eyes and almost immediately drifting off into a heavy, dreamless sleep.

Chapter 24
Monday, 26ᵗʰ December, 2022

On Boxing Day Mum realised my cousin had left some of his presents behind, and so, after Max's morning nap we decided we'd go for a drive over to Paddington to drop them off. After dropping the presents, we were going to pop into Michael and Ally's place to drop off their new toilet seat. The toilet seat is a bit of a long story but let's just say that Michael and I had used the same, as it turned out, dodgy guy to do our bathrooms back in 2019.

I had come home from our wonderful Europe trip to find a new toilet, with a seat that had been stuck on with a messy, gross-looking silicone. Michael ended up with the same seat, stuck on with the same silicone. We both agreed the toilets must have fallen off the back of a truck somewhere. I'd finally paid to have a new one installed just before my surgery, so Mum had paid the same company to install a new one for Michael. I'd wrapped the new toilet seat in Christmas paper for a bit of fun once I had run out of actual presents to wrap.

I brought food and water for Max just in case. The plan was to do the round trip and be home in time to feed him but I guess Christmas had really worn him out because he ended up falling asleep about 5 minutes before we got to Michael and Ally's place. Mum asked if we wanted to go for a drive to Maroubra, one of the beaches about 10 minutes away. I had trained there with my personal trainer (who was an ex Rabbitoh's player) and with my brothers and Uncle Greg many years ago so I thought it would be great to see the old stomping ground. I was a little nervous about Max waking and getting cranky because he was hungry but he slept soundly while we drove along, taking in the beautiful scenery every time we caught a glimpse of the ocean. Rose preferred to stare at the old phone I had given her a SIM card for, and normally I would tell her to put it away and look at the beautiful scenery but I thought she deserved a bit of special treatment after the seven months or so that we had all endured.

Max slept for 45 minutes, the longest he'd ever slept in the car. He was perfectly happy when he woke up, despite the fact he was overdue for lunch. I was nervous about him getting cranky on the drive home and so, at Mum's suggestion, I stopped for sushi before heading to nearby Queen's Park so that everyone could eat.

Max could barely concentrate on his banana because of the fascinating pigeons. I realised, a little sadly, that he'd only ever been to a park once before, when I'd been in hospital six weeks earlier. Rain threatened but didn't eventuate until just after we had walked in the door an hour and a half later. I wasn't surprised that Max was a little overtired when we got home but we had a wonderful adventure and no one had had a nervous breakdown, least of all me.

The next week flew by. Rose and I went shopping for school shoes and to check out the Boxing Day sales. We finally braved the long drive up to the Blue Mountains another day. It was the outing we had been intending to go on with Dani, Andy and Will when they were here. I was nervous about taking Max so far from home in the car but he slept all the way there. We had a wonderful day, stopping for lunch before driving around and looking at the beautiful scenery. Max slept almost all the way home and then happily watched the world go by outside for the last 20 minutes or so. He didn't even cry once.

We were able to make up for lost time with my wonderful friends, as well. We caught up with the Morgans for the first time since Max and baby Isobel had arrived, with the exception of all the wonderful help that Tina had been whilst I was so unwell. I was so thrilled to see that my baby was so confident and chirpy around other people. Baby Isobel actually clapped when she finally met her new friend and I'm pretty sure it went to his head, having a pretty girl making such a fuss over him.

Throughout that week, between Christmas and New Year, we were out almost every day. With each outing I grew more and more confident that maybe Max was going to be just fine. He no longer cried constantly and seemed like such a happy little fellow. He was still growing perfectly and although he was still very much the little mummy's boy he had started to become after my operation, he was also very much a nanna's boy and he thought the sun absolutely shone from his sister, which, quite frankly, I wholeheartedly agreed with.

I was making good progress with my book. There were certain chapters that would make me cry like a baby, reliving some of those moments while they were so raw would make me feel so vulnerable and distraught. I don't know how many times Rose had asked, confused by my suddenly red tear-streaked face, if I was okay. But the answer was finally, yes. I knew I still had a little way to go but for the first time in months I started to realise that I really was going to be okay. Something that I'd feared I would never be again.

I felt so inspired by the number of women who'd reached out to me with their own stories of birth injury and trauma after I'd shared on social media that I was planning to write about my own experiences. I was noticing a theme though: so many of those women felt like they couldn't talk about what they had been through, certainly not the way I was doing by writing about the most intimate type of injuries a woman could experience. It made me sad to think that even in the present day, when the Jetson's car was just about a reality, women were experiencing the same horrific events during and after child birth as what I had been through, and they were too embarrassed and ashamed to talk about it.

One day, when I was reading some of the messages I had been sent by other women about their own traumatic births, I came up with an idea. I decided I was going to start a podcast. I had absolutely no idea where to start, but I knew it was the perfect way to engage with other women and give them a platform to talk about their experiences. I had seen that there were a few podcasts about birth injury and trauma but mine was going to be different. I wasn't sure how exactly, but I'd figure out the details later.

Before getting over-excited and purchasing the long list of electronic thingy-majiggy's I was going to need in order to record my podcast episodes, I decided to once again turn to social media. I had become so passionate about talking to other women about the experience I'd had and, in turn, hearing about their own experiences. Talking to that wonderful woman Michele, who bought my kayak, had really stuck with me. I had been in such a bad way that day, but that chance meeting with a stranger had given me a glimmer of hope. I had talked to her like an old friend, which was ironic really since I hadn't really told my closest friends what I was going through, not the extent of it, anyway. In truth, I made a wonderful new friend that day. She was, and has continued to be, so very inspiring.

I wanted to help other women to feel that glimmer of hope, just like I had felt when I started to share my story. But I knew that in order to succeed with a podcast I would have to set out at least fifteen episodes. I knew I had four or five women already keen to be a part of my new project but I needed more. I was absolutely bursting with ideas and so I started posting on LinkedIn. I was conscious of the fact that I was starting my new job in mid-January and so I didn't have much time to plan and start recording everything. My goal was to have five episodes recorded before I was back at work, and I would then spend nights and a few hours on the weekend doing a new episode each week. Being a few weeks ahead would mean that I could

    But baby, you're worth it!

take time out during school holidays, or if we had plans on a weekend.

The response I received from those LinkedIn posts absolutely blew me away. I had women I had worked with and women I had never met before reaching out. So many women wanted to share their birth stories with me. Two women, one of whom was a close friend, and the other was a lady named Kelly, who had seen one of my posts, wanted to include my story on their podcasts and to be included on mine. That stranger has quickly become one of my biggest supporters. Kelly not only helped me to connect with so many women who were ready to talk about their own experiences of childbirth, she actually took me through the exciting and terrifying process of turning my podcast idea into a reality.

Chapter 25
Saturday,
31st December, 2022

One of the huge lessons I have learned over the months since I had my beautiful little boy is that I should have trusted my instincts. Whilst I was going back and forth in those early weeks, to the nasty midwife at the hospital and those doctors who completely ignored the pain I was in, when my body had been trying to rid itself of the retained placenta. I knew there was something wrong with me. I had been through every kind of test and procedure imaginable in the nine years I was trying to conceive my little Max. A woman does not go through all of that and come out the other end clueless about her own body.

I am so thankful that my mum pushed me to keep going back for answers. I have two beautiful children who were depending on me to get myself better. I am so sad to think that taking care of Max and I caused Mum to lose her own health, but I feel hopeful now. My mum finally seems to be getting better again. Touch wood. The attacks are becoming less frequent and the new medication, mixed with the injections, seem to be making a huge difference. I don't know how I would have survived

But baby, you're worth it!

without her help. I just hope I can be the same kind of mother to my children that she has always been for me.

I'm not sure if I will ever be truly free of the paranoia that still plagues me when I take my little boy out of the house, but I am so much more confident now than I was just a couple of months ago, so who knows? Maybe there will come a day when I will feel confident enough to take him to childcare or even leave him to sleep in his own cot, without me constantly needing to see him and check he is okay. But I guess there are worse things in the world than worrying about your children.

I am excited, but more than a little bit scared, about my beautiful Rose starting high school in a few weeks. I have been trying not to think about it because I know it will make me emotional. The first time I cried about my baby going to high school was when I was pregnant with Max. I had caught sight of one of her daycare photos that hang on the wall in my hallway. I had suddenly realised that she was growing up far too quickly. I blamed the pregnancy hormones back then, but I suspect all parents probably go through something similar, wishing their kids would stay small for a little longer. I am trying to arrange with my new company to push my start date out by a few weeks.

I want to be able to get through my follow-up appointment. I am feeling a bit better each day. I still have a bit of bleeding and I'm starting to wonder if it will ever stop, but I can pick up my little Max, which is huge. I can't wait to drive Rose to and from school for her first couple of weeks of high school. I know that I will have to let her catch the bus at some point, just like her friends, but I am grateful I get to have that special time while she settles in. It also means I will have more time to figure out the whole podcast thing, which is scary but also so very exciting. Maybe one day it will even be a huge success and become a way for me to earn a living while still being able to juggle things like school drop off and baby naps. How great would that be?

I wish I had never allowed an inexperienced doctor to use the forceps to deliver my little boy, I should have insisted on a cesarean as I had originally planned when I had found out I was pregnant, before the doctors had talked me out of it. But I can't go back and so I will continue to hustle. I will keep talking about my experience so that other women will be empowered to make better decisions for themselves and their families.

I'm still more than a little compulsive ... I still have to record every meal and bottle on a notepad. I no longer record every poo that Max does though, and let me tell you, that boy poos A LOT! I still shake those bottles 50 times, but at least I see the humour when Rose mocks me for it now. And do you know what, it turns out that all that shaking with my right arm has toned it up nicely ... I've actually started swapping sides to try and tone my left arm up as well. I might even start dancing around with actual dumbbells soon, or maybe I can get back into my much more rigorous walking and find the arm and leg weights that have been gathering dust in the garage.

I will never stop telling my girls, Rose, and my two nieces, Brittany and Ally, that they must always advocate for themselves. And to educate themselves, about their bodies and about their rights as

But baby, you're worth it!

women in a world that still has a long way to go towards achieving true equality. I had never realised that even the medical system discriminates against women but I have come to see this is very much the case. There is no way men would be ignored and told they were being dramatic when experiencing the devastating amount of pain and trauma that I did over those months.

There is no way a man would have been laughed at as he was delivered the life-altering news that he could no longer hold an erection or some other condition that would alter and destroy him at the very core of what makes him a man. I don't ever want my girls, or *any* woman, to allow some ignorant middle-aged man to laugh, while delivering the news they would never again be able to carry a child within their bodies, as though that concept was some big joke.

I wish I had confided in my close friends. I am so lucky to have a number of strong, supportive women in my inner circle. I realise now that each and every one of them would have been on my doorstep as soon as possible, if only I had asked. Even beautiful friends overseas would have somehow managed to send provisions. But I was so ashamed of my injuries and of the way I was feeling, so sad, scared and overwhelmed. I have never been good at asking for help. I'm too proud and stubbornly independent, just like my mum. I can only hope that if my closest friends and family are ever faced with hurdles of their own that they will know I'm there, in whatever capacity they need me.

I so desperately wish that someone had walked over that day in the parent's room in the shopping centre and asked if I was okay.

I felt so alone that day and truly disconnected. I know several people did see me crying and chose to ignore me. I want to ask you, whether you are a man or a woman, a first-time parent or a grand-parent of 10 beautiful babies — Please, go over! If you see a parent crying as they cradle their screaming baby, please check on them. I'm not saying that a kind word or hug would have instantly healed me that day of everything that was going on, but it would have meant the world to know that someone outside of my little bubble actually cared.

My little family has so much to look forward to next year. We have our week up at Robin's place on the Gold Coast. I have Valentine's Day, Easter egg hunts, a first birthday and a 13th to look forward to, both such special milestones. I have the daunting but exciting task of finding the special woman who will carry and birth my 3rd baby for me — that alone is going to be an epic adventure and I can't wait to tell you all about it. Plus, there will be so many more special moments to share with my loved ones, so many harbourside walks and carpet picnics. Some of it will make me laugh, and I'm sure that some will make me want to pull my hair out and scream, but I'll get through it, and we'll all be okay and most importantly, we will be happy, at least most of the time.

I've just arrived home from Attimo with my special, made-to-order pizza with prawns, ham, mushrooms, garlic and extra cheese. If you look them up, tell them I sent you and ask for the Tabitha special, because that's what my special order is now called. Mum and I will share the pizza while the kids are having pasta and garlic crust pizza to share. Rose has laid out some

          But baby, you're worth it!

towels in the yard, under the clothesline of all places. It's such a glorious evening we decided to bring the carpet picnic outside.

I wish I had waited to go ahead with the operation to fix the prolapse, but at least the worst of it is behind me, finally. I hope that my bleeding will stop at some point. It's been 7 weeks now and I'm still wearing those horrible maternity pads. At least the pain is almost completely gone. I will have to live with these birth injuries forever and I'm still processing that fact. But I'm healing, slowly but surely. It's a case of baby steps, that's for sure. I just need to remind myself that I can no longer flop myself down on my lounge or my bed, because when I do, I am instantly reminded of my injuries. From what I've read, this will probably never change.

I hope my story will help other women who have been through their own nightmare after childbirth to heal, understanding that you're not alone. I see you, and I feel you. So many of us have suffered through these life-altering injuries just because we chose to do what is supposed to be the most natural thing that a woman can do, to give birth to our children. I hope my story will make those of you who are sitting down to write your own birth plan, or even planning your future pregnancies, do your own research and educate yourself about the different methods of assisted births. I wish I had known to do that, to have been able to advocate for my body and my little baby. I thank God, or whoever it is up there, every day, that my little boy wasn't hurt by those forceps, like so many babies are. But for now, it's time to put my phone down and soak up every moment with my beautiful, healthy and happy children.

But before I go, I want to say one last thing. Motherly love is a funny thing. I have been to hell and back this year, I have learned some lessons, some were good and many I could absolutely have gone without. The trauma, pain and suffering have been the worst thing I have ever lived through ... But baby, you're worth it. I would do it all again in an instant, if it meant holding you and your beautiful sister in my heart and in my arms.

THE END

But baby, you're worth it!